The Mouth Is A Coven

a novel

Liz Worth

Copyright © 2022 by Liz Worth

All rights reserved.

Print Edition ISBN: 978-1-958370-05-6

E-book edition ISBN: 978-1-958370-04-9

Manta Press, Ltd.
www.mantapress.com

Cover Design by Tim McWhorter

Author Photo by Lisa East

First Edition

This book is a work of fiction. Names, characters, places and events portrayed within are either the product of the author's imagination or are used fictitiously. Any resemblance to actual persons, living or dead, events, institutions or locales is entirely coincidental.

No part of this book may be reproduced in any form or by any electronic or mechanical means, including information storage and retrieval systems, without written permission from the author, except for the use of brief quotations in a book review.

Acknowledgements

The tone and shape of this novel started in Nancy Kilpatrick's vampire fiction class many, many moons ago. Thank you, Nancy, for your knowledge and encouragement.

Thank you to Heather Babcock, Kia Kotsanis, and Kire Paputts for being early readers of this work and for offering thoughtful feedback and enthusiasm for the story.

Thank you to Ariel Gore's manuscript workshop, and to my fellow participants who took the time to read through various passages and iterations of this novel along the way.

Thank you to Mary and Nelson.

And finally, thank you to Tim McWhorter at Manta Press for making this book a reality.

Prayer: A Prelude

Don't come looking for us, because we're already gone, and the names of people and places have all been changed to protect anyone still living.

Now I'm just a girl in someone else's dream, pointing at a sticky note pasted to a wall and saying, "This is all you need to know about this story."

We never thought it would happen this way. We really believed we could have been chosen for something greater than this. This, which is nothing in the end.

Listen: Someone is calling the quarters—North, South, East, West. I used to do that, too. Now I know better. Besides, those words were chanted so often through these city streets the walls still whisper them back, as if our words live as permanent echoes.

I wish they wouldn't.

Regardless of what brought each of us here, it still seemed so fateful, so fatal. We were His constellation. He moved us around like planets, constructing the perfect aspects, kept us shifting from harsh alignments to slaughtered harmony.

Profit hect morse sa tic perplame

"Praise, protect me from this place."

It's a prayer someone gave me a long time ago, something handed to me off the streets.

What did I need protection from? What is this charm against? If I ever knew, I've long forgotten. Maybe that's why it never seemed to work when I needed it.

Where I'm from, you sometimes feel like you have to cut up words and letters to keep your intentions secret. There are so many ghosts here, around every corner. They listen to everything you're saying. But nothing can really stop them from knowing our true thoughts, feelings. Especially not when you're as intent on knowing some of them as we were. Naïve, naïve. What did we think would happen when we opened doors we couldn't close? Still, this prayer made me feel better, a consolation despite everything that led up to it.

I probably don't need those words anymore, but I don't know if I will ever be able to let them go. You might want to hang onto them, too. Just in case.

1
People Like Us

There is a story in Starling City about a vampire who is on the same level as the gods. So much so we capitalize our letters when we talk about Him. Out of reverence. Out of respect.

The stories say He is very old: As old as this land, which existed before this place was ever called Starling City. None of the stories about Him say whether He sleeps in a coffin, or changes into a bat. None of the stories worry too much about whether or not He can go out in the sunlight, though He doesn't really have to because everyone who loves Him prefers the night, anyway. Everyone meaning people like us. That means me, Julie, and my friend, Blue.

There are stories that say this vampire is a spirit. Or a demon. Or a deity. We prefer the latter, because we know it to be true. His name is Matter, and He has survived here so long because He does not need a body. He can take possession of one when He wants and leave it whenever He is done with it. This is why so many people in Starling City blame the demon Matter for all the missing persons' reports around here.

Matter has been legend on this land for as long as your

mother's mother's mother's mother's mother might even remember. Like any old god, this vampire lives on belief and burnt offerings, the incense-laden rituals that take place in teenage bedrooms. You can go into town and find incantations in His name in old books if you are patient enough to scour the dusty old shops on Palmer Street.

The story we are telling you—that is, Julie and Blue—is the story of belief in real time. If people believe in Matter badly enough, He will come and find them. At least that's the story we always heard.

Around here, people talk about things that happened years ago. They say the soil in the cemetery on Cedar Road had gone black, that the man who'd sanctified the ground had a crow's eye for a heart. It was said that when the dead were buried there, the roots of nearby trees wrapped themselves around the decaying bodies to suck up whatever life was left behind. As winter changed over to spring, the tree blossoms no longer held the youth of new growth, but hung heavy, their petals black with old blood. As spring gave way to the sweat of summer, those trees would glisten, weeping crimson.

Another story tells of the time the moon swallowed the sun and the air grew colder and night clung to the windows and doors, draping itself over rooftops long after morning should have risen. When the sun did finally appear, some of the women refused to walk in the light, waiting only for night to return. Then, they would circle around the perimeter of the town—just dirt roads back then—mouths working around dangerous, unholy words.

The prayers they sent into the wind were wrong. Some versions of the story say these women were sadly mistaken, thought they were speaking to a different deity, something more benevolent than the one we've already mentioned. Others say they knew exactly what they were doing. It doesn't matter anymore, does it? Because either way, they spoke those prayers not to God but to something older, something the rest of the world had forgotten about, something that had crawled down from the darkness and into their dreams.

The story goes that these women had sent out so many prayers night after night that the streets couldn't hold them anymore, and neither could the woods beyond the roads. In the morning, incantations could still be heard, consonants knocking up against windowsills, syllables blowing gently against earlobes. Soon it seemed as though the city itself was uttering foul words, as though the women had willed this place to carry on their work while they hid from daylight. Some people say that those prayers continue, that those are the words you can hear when you're walking home alone late at night and you'd swear there's no one around for blocks.

Back then was also when the children started to go missing from their beds. In their places would be branches and dried roots, earthen things creeping across the bedsheets. People would check their doors, windows. They looked for footsteps leading in and out of their homes. There was never any evidence of a break-in or struggle, as though the children had all let themselves out.

Some felt it was the influence of the moon, others the

spell that the women had cast—or cursed—over this place. No child who went missing that year was ever found during any search.

Instead, they each came back on their own, a year and a day after their disappearances. They let themselves in at night and snuck back into their beds as though they had never left. But none returned quite the same. Something had changed them. At supper time they would speak in strange tongues, a language that might have been the layers of prayers of the women who had walked Starling City's streets so long before. Some were found with their hands around the necks of cats and dogs, squeezing hard. Once in a while, their parents would find their children's beds filled with dirt and mud and sticks, the bottoms of their feet caked with debris. Evidence that they ran through the woods all night and returned before sunup.

"Which of us descended from those children?"

You would ask yourself this, if you were born and raised in Starling City like we were. And these are stories that every kid who grows up here learns. Even the blades of grass hum these legends because everything that grows here has its roots seeded in the buried dead beneath the city's surfaces. The moss and mushrooms grow as prayers that everyone who grows up here knows how to listen to.

What sets us all apart as we grow older is those who choose to keep listening, and those who remember, versus those who don't. Because there are, of course, people around here who say these are urban myths and nothing more. Kids forget and grow into adults who dismiss the old gods as superstitions, or the legends as collective dreams no one can quite remember the details of. The ones who keep these stories close and alive are the ones who know that if you stand on a street corner and snap your fingers three times on a windy day, a ghost might appear. We are the ones who disappear into the woods and look for dead girls to guide them to hidden graves where their gods may sleep.

To the ones who remember, the stories of Starling City are religion. To people like us, these stories are as real as blood and bone.

2
Strange Kiss

The magic doesn't really start until Blue and Julie meet.

Before then, Blue spends some afternoons standing at the corner of King and Cumbrae. He comes here once a week, at least, and points his finger at drivers stopped at the traffic lights. No one is ever sure how to react to this, or what it means—if it means anything at all. Sometimes, the guy who runs the barbershop nearby pops his head outside and tells Blue to piss off. "You're scaring off my customers, you little creep. Get a life."

Chaos magicians just laugh in times like these. What a compliment to be called a creep in this context. Understand Blue's frame of mind: He likes the life he has, imagines that just by stirring fear, or questions, or whatever feelings arise by his simple, single pointed finger, that he is opening some kind of portal. But Blue would never lose track of time out there: There are always things to get home to later, like TV specials about UFOs and heavy metal music videos and his books on vampires and witchcraft.

There are a lot of witches in Starling City. They scream into empty jars, seal them up, and then leave them around town. Vessels trapping anger, energy, rage, words — whatever they want to unleash and then capture. The jars get left out for people to find, or to be broken when the Starling City winds knock them over. Blue collects any jars he can find to take home with him. Alone, he breathes it all in, every bottle a strange kiss.

Blue's room is covered in old newspaper articles full of photos of dead animals, or what was left of them: severed heads, paws. They used to find decapitated birds by the river. Blue's favourite story is the one about a goat's head and hooves found on the steps of a church. Eventually, these things started happening so often that it wasn't even news anymore, so the papers just stopped writing about it. But that doesn't mean the deaths are over. Cats' eyes still end up in people's mailboxes. Wings—mostly pigeons', it seems—are stuffed into the black bars of basement windows. People see things like this all the time on their way to work in the early mornings. It's always morning, when these discoveries are made.

Some people, like Blue, think they're ritual sacrifices. Others are convinced it's connected to something else. There are a lot of unsolved murders in Starling City, a lot of missing persons, too. Mysteries, like any city. Except that Starling City isn't like any other place.

Every night, Blue lights a red candle in his window, a signal for something he hopes is always watching. Inside the apartment, Blue is often alone after dark. His mother lives here, too, though she's rarely home. When she is, she's gone by five o'clock. That's when happy hour starts at the Blue Lagoon.

In the kitchen, Blue opens a can of pasta in red sauce.

He enjoys watching the soft, meat-filled cushions slide out into a bowl. He imagines the sauce is blood, bright and alive with the memories of the body it once flowed through. It reminds him of the movies that come on TV after midnight, the ones he loves to watch with all the lights turned off. His favourites are the ones where the characters are bitten by creatures that have risen from the earth.

Blue believes that if he were to become a vampire, he would see flashes of his victims' lives rush before his eyes as he took their blood into his body. Wouldn't that be cool? He asks himself and answers back that yes, it would be really fucking cool.

Blue doesn't bother heating his pasta. He likes it room-temperature. Truthfully, he would rather not have to eat at all. Bodily habits are embarrassing to him and only serve as reminders of his mortality and ordinariness. Blue wants to be supernatural. He wants to be something Other, something outside of himself.

The thing he wants to be most is a vampire. In everything he's seen and read and imagined, vampires never get old, and never die. They are untouched by everything Blue sees as normal and boring. They don't get old, and they don't have day jobs—something Blue has actively avoided so far. They stay up all night and sleep and all day, a schedule that suits Blue just fine.

Blue believes—no, he knows—his life would be easier, better even, if he was something other than human. And he's trusting that all of his spells and rituals and arcane workings will someday, somehow, all come together.

Soon, soon, he tells himself. One of these days, his magic will work.

He sinks into the couch. The ashtray on the side table is piled so high he can smell it. He puts it on the floor, spilling ash and butts as he does so. He doesn't bother to clean it up. The apartment is always a mess, anyway. By the time his mother comes back, she will be so drunk she won't even notice. If she does, she will assume she made the mess herself. Blue flips through the channels. There is nothing on today. He eats his pasta fast, barely tasting it. When he's done, he lights a cigarette, flicks the ash into his empty bowl where the remaining streaks of red sauce catch the black and white remnants of cheap tobacco.

Blue falls asleep on the couch, something he rarely does because it is usually where his mother sleeps when she bothers to come home. She never stays in her bedroom because clothes and shoes and purses and wire hangers and hairbrushes cover her bed. You cannot walk across the floor without stepping on something. The cockroaches don't even scatter anymore when you turn the lights on in there. The roaches know it is their room now.

Blue dreams of a film scene made real. In it, he's wrapped in the embrace of a man who wears the wings of a bat. They are on a street corner, tangled up in each other. It should be nighttime, but the sun is out. People are walking by. No one stops to intervene or to offer help.

Blue was never held by his father. At least, not that he can remember. In his dream, he imagines that this is what it would feel like to be loved like that. The intimacy of someone's powerful arms around him, the strength of another man's body pressing against his. Blue closes his eyes, his dream-body heavy, wanting to give itself over to rest. Blue can't keep his eyes open. The man tells him, "It's okay. Just let yourself go to sleep." Blue nuzzles his head on the man's shoulder and feels something wet against his neck. The vampire drinks deeply. Blue dips further down into his dream before coming up again, changing scenes without transition the way dreams do sometimes.

Now, he's the one with the bat wings and hungry throat. Except he's not as gentle as the vampire before. No, Blue is one who rages through the night. He tries to grab at anyone who passes by, but they dodge him, evade his touch. Finally, he gets a girl in his grip but wakes before he can get a taste of her. He tries to go back to sleep to continue dreaming, but he can't pick up the thread again. His only reveries after come in fits and starts of odd images and minor arguments.

In the morning, Blue's red candle, which he forgot to blow out, has melted down on his windowsill. The wax looks like long drips of blood.

3
Proof of Ghosts

There are other things Blue does to pass the time. Like talking to the ghost of his sister, Samantha. She's the one who taught him how to see spirits in the first place.

If you walk by yourself along certain streets at certain times of night, you can see the ghosts of Starling City. The trick is to stare straight ahead, with eyes slightly unfocused, and let your peripheral vision do the work.

Ghosts don't like it when you stare at them straight on. That's why they're so hard to see. Some people are looking too hard for proof. There is no need for it. People want to be impressed by spirits who don't always want to be seen. That's how misunderstanding leads to misbelief.

The Golden Grocery parking lot has some of the best hauntings, full of lurching apparitions. Blue and Samantha would sometimes sit on a parking stop away from the store entrance, where it wasn't as crowded with shoppers and buggies. There, they would smoke cigarettes and wait for the action to start.

Now it's Sam that Blue watches for. He says her name like a mantra: Sam. Sam. Sam. There's a spiritual law in Starling City that says if you call upon your ancestors, they are obliged to answer.

Sam loved the dead. She pasted pictures of the deceased on her bedroom walls. Mostly poets, rock stars, but sometimes she also cut handsome faces from the newspapers, victims of local tragedies. Sam would kiss their papery lips at night. Sometimes, she would take herself out to a diner and sit in a booth, pretending someone was with her. A beautiful face from her bedroom walls, visiting from beyond.

Blue never saw her do those things, but he read about it later in her diary. Not that she had so many secrets from him. No, she always trusted her little brother, even when she started sneaking out at night. Sometimes Sam would come home and crawl into Blue's bed instead of her own. On those nights she'd be crying, or sick from cheap beer. She would reach for him, wanting to be held: "I'm scared," she would say.

"Of what?" Blue wanted to know.

The stories were the same, but different: There was the man who followed her home one night, and the knife her new boyfriend carried. There was the fight she had with her friends, and the things they all thought they saw in the forest where they went drinking most nights.

Sometimes she didn't tell Blue anything, just sobbed quietly beside him. If she got sick in the toilet, Blue would wait in the hall to make sure she was okay. Their mom would never have noticed, if she was even home at all.

One night, Sam still wasn't back by morning. A truck driver had spotted her body on the side of the road at around six a.m. They said her heart had stopped beating on her way out of the woods. The edge of trees is thick by the roadside. One of her friends came forward to say that they'd all been there the night before.

"There are witches in those trees," Sam had once told Blue. And then, "No, actually. That's not entirely accurate: The trees are witches."

Sometimes, Blue takes the bus out to the edges of town and then walks along the perimeter of the woods, where the roadside gravel meets the forest. There, he tries to find the thing that stopped his sister's heart, but most of the time, the grounds are silent and the trees keep their secrets to themselves.

At home, Samantha's ghost sometimes looks at him with wet, sick eyes. Did you know your eyes grow larger once you become a spirit? People always said Blue and Samantha had the same eyes. It was the only thing that gave them away as siblings. Otherwise, Sam's face was sharp and narrow, whereas Blue's stayed round, babyish. Even as he got older, Blue always looked younger, where Samantha could pass for a few years beyond her age. She also had the dark hair that Blue pined for. It was Samantha who taught him how to colour it himself, covering over his plain brown hair with the cheap blue-black dye he's known for today. His hair is why everyone calls him Blue: it leaves an indigo tint when light hits it.

Now, Samantha's eyes are so big they look painted on, oil on canvas left to dry for another hundred years. She is often crying when she shows up. Sometimes she can speak, and other times she can't. Blue often asks her what's wrong.

The last time they talked, she said, "I know where you're going to go one day, and I know you're not going to find what you're looking for once you get there."

4
Chalk Circle

Blue does not have a job. He has never had a job because he has never wanted one, and never had to get one because of the pills his mom takes. She goes from one doctor to another and gets piles of prescriptions that collect in her purse. She takes the pills for a pain that Blue is sure only exists in her soul, not her body, for he has never known his mom to be injured in her life. Some of the pills get you moving, and some make you slow down. And the rest make you fall asleep and forget everything you ever knew about yourself. The latter are his mom's favourites, which is why she never notices when any of her other pills go missing.

Blue's friends like all the pills, too, but their favourites are the yellow ones that make your body feel light and fill your lungs with giggles. Or the white pills that make your mind zoom. Those are the best for staying up all night. They're all good and strong; whichever you take depends on what you're ready to feel. Blue sells them for five bucks each to friends like Kevin Dyer. Kevin lives in the suburbs and always has cash.

It's a forty-five minute bus ride from Blue's apartment to Kevin's place, which is a bungalow he shares with his mom.

The ride is usually worth it. Blue can make fifty to sixty bucks, easy, off Kevin and his friends, who are all suburban goth kids with their Hot Topic dresses and soft bodies, signs of the well-fed.

It's Saturday, which means Kevin has barely stopped partying. He goes all weekend and whoever can keep up with him is welcome to stay. There is always someone at his house. His mother is a flight attendant and hardly ever home. When she is, she feels so guilty for being gone that she lets Kevin do whatever he wants and orders food for all his friends. There is a stain on the living room carpet from where Kevin puked up pepperoni pizza after doing too many tequila shots last year. A memento of the times they've had.

Today Blue arrives to find a gorgeous girl, all long black curls and thick eyeshadow, sprawled across the floral print sofa, colours clashing against the ink of her tight leather pants. He's met her before but can't remember her name. He knows she's a poseur but still thinks she's hot.

Kevin puts his arm around Blue and says, "I was just about to call you," because surely they are bonded through the telepathy of getting high.

Blue holds out a Ziploc bag of pills and says, "Let me know who wants what." Megadeth is playing on the stereo, and two guys, Daryl and Jess, are rolling a skunky joint that they've half-spilled into the carpet because they're already more beers in than they can count.

"I'm tired," the girl on the couch says. Her words sound like a purr, rumbling and drawn out. Kevin reminds Blue that the girl's name is Zoriah, and when Blue says hello to her, she just smiles and looks away. The girls that hang out at Kevin's are always different from the ones Blue sees downtown; the downtown girls will look you in the eye every time and aren't afraid for their faces to be a little bit ugly.

Blue gives Zoriah a pill to perk her up. Kevin takes one of everything, which is typical. Daryl and Jess don't even look at what they take from the bag, just pay their money and pop the first pills they touch.

It takes about twenty minutes for everything to kick in and that's when there's more to do at Kevin's than party. Even the suburban kids aren't so far from the city to not know the legends. Sometimes they live for the legends more than anyone else.

When Kevin nods, everyone knows it's time to go to the basement. There, on the unfinished concrete floor, they draw a white chalk circle. Kevin lights the candles. Daryl and Jess start to hum. The song is something that rises from the earth, a song of the dead that lives on the lips of anyone willing to keep it alive.

5
To Summon a Demon: Lesson 1

Breathe, focus. Somehow it's easier to summon demons when the blood is full of booze and pills, substances that make bodies open portals, removing barriers and vulnerabilities.

Breathe again. Focus. Think of the word FLOW.

Focus on the image of a man with the head of a bull, horns high.

Focus on the image of sharp teeth sinking into your wrist. Now, you're next.

Sigh like you enjoy the pain. (Zoriah moans, runs her hands over her body.)

Focus on the image of a white feather floating down from the sky. Count backwards from twenty. See each number flash in your mind's eye.

Count yourself back into the dream you had the night before.

Someone from that dream will return now to the circle.

Open your eyes: Whose dream are we in today?

Not that anything ever happens when they sit in a circle like this. Well, there was that one time when they played light as a feather, stiff as a board, and Kevin became convinced he had levitated. But then they were all so high no one could really say that it happened for sure. It would become another suburban legend about the kids who practiced witchcraft on Delaney Street.

Then there was that other time when they were all high on magic mushrooms and they swore they saw something in the corner, Baphomet with his wings and horns standing on curved hind legs. There was another girl hanging around then, Jenn, who wrote it all out on Kevin's bedroom wall later:

Impaired, these skin folds cut corners
  In pairs, in thirds, adding up like this: 2times6minus999screams
3x3x3 = HEAVENANDHELLANDMYHEAD
This is a memory lapse. My organs are potentially fatal.
8 = These eyes
I am impaired. I am damaged, but I know the key. The key is 3. The key is in 3. The key is in me.
  We will all die here. We will all die here. We will all die here.
  The number 7 means: Trust your nervous system
  543:9—this is the ratio to abide by. Do you know why? Because there are telepaths among us.
  I know what's buried here. It lies in schematic drawings, it's waiting for your disturbances. It can hear mine and that's why I will die first unless I invent the number 6. We think we know the number 6 but right now it's only a symbol, nothing more than a symbol, but it hasn't been invented yet.
  The definition of 6 has not been created.
  My time is running out unless I write this down. If I write the

following problem down, then 6 will exist and we will all be solved:

Eagles divide the number 9 + years at birth + 867 = MY EYES WILL SEE

Fuck this memory lapse fuck this memory lapse oh somebody please help me help me help me

But did it happen, did it really?

Did it matter? Sometimes devotion is enough. Blue and his friends draw chalk circles on the floor in the hopes of summoning something. The hope is always enough.

So many people (wrongly) assume that the point of magic is to get something. Spiritual acts are rooted in devotion: the better you worship, the better you feel. The more serious you take something, the more your friends look up to you. The one who takes it the furthest is the one who will be remembered.

The act of the ritual feeds a hunger and belief. It sustains against the boredom of a life that offers little variety.

Define devotion:

    1. Loyalty or enthusiasm. Love that manifests into a sense of duty. (Did you know that the usage of the term "devotion" has been in steady decline since the 1800s? Where will the old gods go if no one stays committed to them?)

    2. Spiritual observance. Religious worship. (Do you have the courage to give yourself over to something completely? Do you know what it means to surrender to the duty of magic?)

    3. Prayers. Incantations. Chants. The observance of an unseen world. (Do you know the

secrets of the moon? Do you know how to read into the darkest folds of the lunar phases? Do you know how to use your words to change the reality you see around you?)

Blue wakes the next morning on a floral bedspread, big red roses and purple lilacs to match the upholstery in the living room. Kevin's mother's room, with its neatly lined perfume bottles and costume jewellery tucked neatly into a glass box on the dresser. All made to look more expensive than it is.

Blue's shirt is off. Dried red wax sticks to his chest: The body is an altar, a place for spells and enchantments.

What kind of magic did they work last night? Blue can't remember now. He tugs lightly at the wax stuck to the hairs around his nipples. He likes the feel of the gentle sting. He knows from experience the wax will melt off in a hot shower. Blue runs his hand through his hair; his head aches just slightly. He pats his pockets and finds his smokes, has a vague memory of Kevin giving him a whole pack from his carton.

Zoriah is on the other side of the bed, fully clothed. It's an enormous bed, king-size. Blue had never seen a bed so big before he ever set foot in Kevin's house.

Kevin's asleep in the chair in the corner. The window looks into the laneway out back, a flat expanse of beige concrete. The landscape is an altar, too, the entire city waiting for the right spell to be spoken.

Everyone is still sleeping when Blue takes the bus back home. Green lawns glow in the late-morning sun. Blue leans his head against the window and puts on his earphones, presses play. The tape in his Walkman grinds out a dark, slinky song. Secretly, Blue likes sunny days like this, even though he would never admit it to anyone. The way the light leaks gold onto everything it touches, the way it warms Blue's skin as it presses through to him.

Back at home, Blue runs the water as hot as he can stand it and then steps into the shower. He likes the way the steam rises around him, like fog. The bathroom tiles are gray with soap scum and black mould grows between them, as it does behind and beneath the various bottles of shampoo that have collected in the four corners of the bathtub. Most bottles have just a little left in each—too much to throw away, too little to pour into your hand. Blue doesn't have the patience to tip a bottle over and wait for the shampoo to ooze to the other end, so he lathers the bar of soap between his hands instead and takes it to his hair. The soap makes his hair coarse. It will dry in tufts and teases, which Blue will run his fingers through to make it wild, standing up on ends like Robert Smith's.

The shower washes away last night's candle wax and the residue of the pills and booze that keep Blue's mind fuzzy at the edges. He stands under the hot water long after all the soap has rinsed away, running his hands over his body, feeling the parts of himself where his bones stick out from beneath his skin.

Blue takes a towel off the rack. It's gone through the washing machine so often that it's frayed at the edges. The towel is so old that it looks dirty, even though it's clean. He hugs it around himself and ignores the dust that sticks to his wet feet, the pebbles that lodge between his toes, as he pads back into his room. He lays back on his bed and closes his eyes. The sun is in a different place in the sky now and when Blue wakes from his nap, it will be even deeper into the horizon, signaling the late afternoon.

This is the worst part of the day sometimes, for Blue—waiting for the night to come. Especially on a Sunday, when things are quieter and a lot of the shops close early, or don't even open at all. There is so much time and space to cover and not enough to do within it all. He presses play on his stereo and turns up the volume, Al Jourgensen's gravel-torn voice filling his room. Blue lights the candles that collect on his desk. Black and white wax stains the carpet. The candles have spilled over onto books and papers. One has devoured half an ashtray and its dusty contents. Blue likes the mess he's made.

One candle on Blue's desk hisses and pops, loosening a fresh stream of wax. Blue stands, then walks in a circle. He imagines the circle can become a door. For what? Whatever may rise. Blue then kneels down again, spits into his hand. This is what ritual can be: Power through bodily fluids. The mouth is a coven of words, a cauldron of intentions. Whatever prayers you speak or wishes you make build energy within the caves of your teeth and the floods of your sputum.

Blue rubs his saliva on the melting candle, the one that hissed for his attention. Spirits speak in many ways, fire being one of them.

Blue watches the flame for a beat, then sends out an

invitation to any spirits who may be near: "Tell me something," he says. "What is it you want to say today?"

6
Turtlenecks

Julie's hair is thick with the smell of grease. She loosens her ponytail, and the odour falls around her shoulders, a shawl woven from the last eight hours. Julie works at the Shamrock Pub and Saturdays are always busy. She hates it, but weekend shifts make the best tips. Julie slips her arms into her leather jacket. Her hands and wrists are tired from carrying plates and pints, and the stiff leather shoes they make her wear at work pinch her feet. But it's Saturday, and Julie will forget it all in a couple more hours.

Julie lives in a walk-up above a dilapidated convenience store. The rent is cheap and the owners like her because she's quiet, unlike some of the other tenants whose units explode with shouts in the middle of the night. Sometimes there are strange people waiting in the stairwell, looking for the guy next door. Sometimes there are cops. But it's all Julie can afford on a server's wage and it's not all bad. There's a small laundry room at the end of the hall and a beautiful old oak tree that grows outside the building. The oak's branches have grown close enough to Julie's bedroom window that they sometimes tap against the glass. It's something that Julie finds reassuring, friendly, even. Sometimes she smiles out at the tree, enjoying its colourful leaves in the warm seasons and its long, bony fingers in the cold ones. It's spring now, and the buds are coming out. In another week or two, green leaves will be fluttering hello and goodbye as Julie comes and goes.

In her bedroom, Julie takes off her clothes. First she removes her socks. She lets her hot, stinging toes sink into the cool fibers of the shag carpet. Next, her black pants come off, and then her turtleneck. Julie always wears black turtlenecks to work, even when it's summer. The better to hide the bites and bruises that loiter on her neck and collarbone.

Julie pauses now to look at herself in the mirror. The sun is going down and the golden light dances between the branches outside her window. She runs a hand over two fading purple spots on her neck and remembers the mouth of the man who made them two nights before. Every bruise a memory, every bite a sweet agony. To pretend like this is such a tease. Julie is always looking for the real thing but can never find it: Teeth strong enough to break the skin without effort, a stranger's deep thirst to drain her.

Julie is one of many in Starling City who hold fantasies of immortality and power. Julie lives for the depth of midnight and craves the dampness of the dark basement bars she frequents. She seeks obscure clubs and strange faces in the hopes that the rumours she's always heard about who and what lives in the shadows of Starling City are true. She works her wishes around the idea of escape: Escape from a life of work, the mundane realities of rent payments and errands and aging. Julie watches old Dracula movies as stories of hope. She doesn't see them as fiction, but as veiled truths that promise an alternate route.

All she needs to do is become something that she's not. Even if it means doing things that most people wouldn't dare try. What will it feel like to find that kind of danger, finally? Looking at herself in the mirror still, she plays with the shape of her mouth, tilting her head back to pretend her face is full of fangs. She smiles at her reflection, then steps away to change into a t-shirt and jeans before taking her laundry down the hall.

The back window of the laundry room looks out over a row of broken-down bungalows. Beyond that, the city rises, stretches into a ridge of trees. The woods thickly lined, a curtain daring to be parted. Julie likes to haul herself up on the washing machine so she can look out the window while she waits for her wash to go through. No one else in the building is ever in the laundry room on a Saturday. Saturdays in Starling City are for partying, not cleaning. She doubts some of her neighbours even bother to wash their clothes at all. Alone, Julie can stare out the window with no one asking her what she's looking at. Though the better question would be: What is she looking *for*?

You have to stare long enough into the woods to let your eyes adjust to the darkness beyond the windowpanes. Then, you can see how the bare, black trees rub their branches together in the wind, restless fingers, wandering hands. Reaching, calling: "Come, come."

The laundry room is small, just enough to fit a washer

and dryer together. The machines are almost flush against each other. Julie can rest her back on the pale green wall. The metal of the washing machine is cold, and her bony ass digs into its surface. She likes the way it rumbles beneath her. She lets her body relax, allows herself to be jostled by the motion.

The sun is almost completely gone from the sky now. Julie likes it when the night falls. It means the woods have more time to be themselves.

Sometimes, you can hear someone screaming back there—a long, single sound, cold as a needle. There are all kinds of stories about what happens in those woods. Julie chooses to only believe in the ones she likes best: That there is a forgotten god who can turn old women young again; that there still stands an old house that was once used for the wrong kind of magic; that those woods are where Julie might find something she's been looking for her whole, young life:

A vampire.

Julie leaves her laundry to roll around in the dryer while she takes a shower. She leans against the bathroom tiles and watches the steam rise around her: Graveyard fog, autumn mist, hag's breath. She lathers shampoo through her hair, scrubs the day off her face until her skin is red and tender. She takes an extra moment to let the water run over her body after everything is wiped clean.

Julie clears steam from the mirror and looks at herself, hard. Hair dripping, skin a little dark under the eyes. She counts her scars: One, two, three, four. The places were bites and kisses sometimes turned into something more. The places where Julie held a blade to her skin and said "drink."

And those places became openings big enough for something else to crawl through, where seeds were planted and blossomed into a black-and-red-bloomed mantra: There's more to life than what you see. There's more, there's more, there's more.

Julie leaves her dry laundry to sit in the basket. She will fold it tomorrow, when she's tired and hungover and her body will still be full of music from the night before.

She makes a grilled cheese sandwich and opens a can of baked beans. The pan is hot and the bread and butter sizzle. Julie watches the cheese melt. She spoons out a small pile of beans to eat at room temperature. The kitchen is too small for a microwave. Julie sits down on the couch with her food, turns on the TV and presses play on the VCR. The same tape is always in the player: *The Hunger*, with David Bowie. Julie rarely watches it past the opening scene, just rewinds it over and over to see Peter Murphy writhe in a cage over a smoky club.

Stop, rewind, play.

The club in the movie is huge and doesn't look much like the ones she goes to in Starling City. They carry names you'd expect them to have given the types of places they are: The Lair, the Spider, the Vixen. Names that imply—or at least try to—atmospheres of danger and darkness and seduction. Each of them are small, concealed affairs. But that doesn't matter to Julie. To her, these places are the centre of the world, the best thing Starling City's got going on. It's her version of the movie scene she's watching now. On the screen, the club's blue lights hit Peter Murphy's cheekbones and Julie wonders if she looks as spectacular when she dances.

Stop, rewind, play.

The camera pans to the crowd and Julie takes in a sea of black leather and red lips, fishnet stockings and tight miniskirts.

Stop, rewind, play.

It's what Julie feels like she's doing when she goes through her closet. Always the same clothes, the same looks. Her tips are good on Saturdays but the pub has been slow the rest of the week lately. The spring rains have kept people indoors, reminding them too much of the winter the city is still shaking off. Julie pulls on her favourite black tank top, faded from too many washes. It doesn't quite match her skirt. In the dark no one will notice.

Leaning into her mirror, Julie pulls long, thick lines around her eyes and coats her eyelashes with inky black mascara. Sigil magic disguised as makeup. Mouth soaked in red lacquer. Jacket on, Julie locks her apartment door and walks back downstairs.

Outside, the moon is a crone, tongue waning and spine curved. A hunched watcher, its light barely enough to throw Julie's shadow across the sidewalk as she waits for the bus that will take her to King Street.

7
Everything a Spell

If you are looking for a vampire in Starling City, King Street is the place to start. There are other options, of course. But even if you can't find the real deal on King Street, you can at least find someone willing to pretend for a little while.

To find them, you need to know about the unmarked clubs that are past the pawn shops, south of the boarded-up storefronts. Look for the red lights that hang above black doors.

Tonight Blue counts dead rats on his way to King: One, two, three, four. One has a severed head, mauled by a cat. Blue crouches down to look at this one, wanting to see what's inside.

Then he stops to look at his reflection in the side mirror of a parked car. Blue pulls a tube of lipstick from his pocket, paints his mouth with an invitation of burnt orange and anticipation.

Blue always knows it's going to be a good night when the streets are alive with black leather and torn denim, wind punctured by spiked heels. He can hear people coming from all directions, silver jewelry dripping off wrists and necks, earrings jangling, buckles and chains jingling from their boots and belts and jackets. People stop to huddle in doorways to share cigarettes and flasks, everyone nodding to each other, knowing they are all going to the same places to look for the same things.

You have to walk with your head high around here. Confidence is survival in a neighbourhood like this. But sometimes, you see someone fall: A heel catches in the sidewalk, or someone slips on the dancefloor. Pulled like thread through the eye of a needle.

It's how Blue feels when he sees Julie on the dance floor later. Falling, like the music that's crashing around them in waves. Pulled like a thread, at mercy to Julie's arms and hands that move to the beat as though she's digging up bones. Blue has seen her here before. She's always alone, like him. He likes the thinness of her wrists, and the purple tint in her hair. He likes that the length of her hair stops just below her ears, leaving her long, slender neck exposed.

Blue doesn't always have money in his pocket to drink, to pay for the courage he needs to talk to her. But today, the cash from Kevin Dyer's party last weekend is heavy in his pocket. Blue buys two glasses of wine, walks up to the girl. Her eyes are closed when he gets to her. He taps her on the shoulder but she doesn't notice, just keeps dancing.

Blue doesn't know that this is Julie's favourite song. To interrupt it is impossible.

When the song is over, she sees him and smiles.

They sit together in a booth near the back of the club. The smoke hangs low in the air. The ceiling so close you can reach up and touch it if you're tall enough. By this time of night, the room is so moist with sweat that it collects in beads, drips back down to the floor. Wet enough to slip. In the next booth, a girl pulls tarot cards for five dollars a reading. She crosses her fingers under the table, lets her legs rest too closely against anyone who sits with her. Julie glances back at her, curious. The girl licks her lips and shows her teeth. She leans over and says, "Anyone can be a witch if they try hard enough."

Everything a spell, and everything in its time. "You want to get some air?" Blue asks. Julie goes to the bathroom first. By this time of night, one of the toilets is overflowing, like usual, and the water is leaking into the hallway. Julie waits in line for the one working stall. On the walls, people have written names and curses, spells and prayers. The name Matter flashes back at her in thick, black letters.

Matter, to whom Julie builds altars for each night.

On the toilet, Julie lets her hand linger a little longer as she wipes, pressing harder than she needs to into the desires of her body.

Out back behind the club are stacks of salvaged milk crates where people sit and smoke and whisper the secrets that can't be heard over the relentless throb of the music inside. There, Blue holds out a glass of wine, purple under the soft light that hangs over the backdoor. Julie drinks faster than she wants to. She folds herself against Blue, rests her head against the warm half-moon of his neck and shoulder.

What happens in those soft spaces where sighs are left

on skin? What happens in those moments that are as gentle as breath? Silent states that hiss and pop with a person's hunger for attention, a deficit of past affections.

Blue can't wait like this for long, with the girl's head so close to his, her mouth—wet cherry mouth covered with cheap lipstick—teasing in the margins of his gaze. His fingers twitch. Testing her hand to see if it will hold. Nervous, he flits with the sleeve of Julie's jacket instead, sees a tattoo there on the bone of her wrist: A crescent moon and star. Its edges are sharp, and Blue wonders if he could prick his fingers on its points.

"I like this," Blue says, running his finger across the black crescent.

Julie nods into the crook of his neck. "Thank you. I can make you one, if you want."

"Really?" Blue asks. "You know how?"

"Uh-huh," Julie says. "I did this one myself. Do you know what it means?"

Blue shakes his head so Julie tells him about moons and stars. She tells him about the magic that she creates. The name Matter appears on her lips, a title that reverberates through the alley. Julie and Blue honour the spirit of the moment before speaking again. Their words are light, spattered with the rumours they've heard, the things they've seen scrawled on bathroom stalls, the books they've read over and over, asking: Could this be real? Could this be really, really, real?

"I want to feel real," Julie says, and tucks herself against Blue's neck again when the silence returns. Blue's fingers slip around Julie's hands. "You feel real to me," Blue says. And then: "Looks like you need another drink," and he points to her empty wine glass that she doesn't remember finishing. Another favourite song creeps out from underneath the backdoor. "Shall we?" Blue asks, pulling Julie inside for more dancing.

As Blue and Julie's feet move, they think of Matter and the underworld that writhes beneath them. The entire club does, everybody silently calling on spirits, raising the dead of Starling City. A pout of black lipstick is an invocation. A long red nail across a taut cheek is a hidden agenda.

The floor is unhallowed, covered with spilled booze and tears and the humidity of desire. Julie steps and slips, falls down. Blue reaches for her, pulls her to him. Laughs it off with her when he knows she's okay, pulled clean through the eye of the needle. Time to go home.

They start a summoning as they ascend the stairs to Julie's apartment. Julie tells Blue some of her favourite magic tricks: Recite poetry to the sky. Throw your head all the way back as you laugh so as to expose the throat. Count your pulse to thirteen and then start over. Learn to listen to the ways the trees rub together in the wind. Slip a piece of quartz crystal under your tongue and gag on the vibrations it sends into every word.

Inside, Julie pulls out her kit, lays India ink and a needle out on the coffee table. "Ready?" she asks Blue. Psychic TV play out a low drone from the stereo in the corner. Blue smokes a cigarette and watches Julie poke the needle in and out. It hurts a little and Blue likes that. A drop of blood runs down his wrists. He wipes it with his pinky finger and takes it to his tongue. "How does it taste?" Julie asks.

"You want to try it?" Blue says. Julie does. When the next drop falls, she dares a taste, closes her eyes as though it's the best thing she's ever tasted.

"There, done," Julie says, sitting back and admiring the moon and star on Blue's wrist. He wanted it in the same place as Julie's. Swollen and red at the edges, the tattoo winks and throbs up at Blue. "I love it," he says, and leans into Julie to meet her mouth.

It's nearly two in the morning and neither of them are tired. Julie pulls out a big white sheet from her closet. On it she has painted a black snake eating its tail. The snake creates a circle to sit within. Julie spreads the sheet across the floor. "Let's try something else now," Julie says.

They light black and white candles and line them up on the coffee table, turning off all the other lights. Julie plays the Psychic TV record again, a recorded ritual. Can't hurt to have the help of someone else's magic, can it?

Julie pulls out a knife she keeps under the couch. The blade is as gentle as each of their mouths, lightly prying open the skin to see what's inside. Blue and Julie peer into the wounds, a search for the words placed within, the ones that will help call them home towards something much more sacred than what they've seen so far. Blood stains the sheets, a loose pattern of dots. Proof of what's real.

They chant Matter's name. Their voices work in tandem, creating a velvet whisper. Even though they speak softly, their words expand and balloon, filling the room, stretching throughout the apartment.

There's a story in Starling City that says the old gods wake when you call them. What does the call sound like? How do they know what to listen for? And do you ever think that the gods are the ones controlling it all: That they place the right words within you, to be released at the right time, tasted through tiny cuts. Incisions made delicately. Razorblade traces offered to warm, waiting mouths.

Blue starts to hum. The hum turns into a wordless song, which gets devoured when Julie kisses his mouth. She's soft and warm. Blue's body responds. Their hips press towards each other, tongues tracing the shapes of curves and bones.

An hour later, the candles have burned lower, and the moon is in another part of the sky. "How will we know if Matter heard us?" Blue asks when he and Julie break apart.

Julie looks around. "I think we would know," she says. "There would be a smell, or a feel to the room. An energy in the air. Wouldn't there?"

Blue has felt deity before but none as big or important as this one. He decides Matter hasn't come, assuming it would be obvious otherwise. "Let's try again tomorrow," Blue says.

In bed, Julie and Blue kiss again, lightly at first, then harder, deeper. They are both down to their t-shirts and underwear. Julie's heart skips whenever their toes touch beneath the sheets. She closes her eyes and tries to sleep. It's hard when her body is this electric, full of lightning and white noise.

8
Seasons

It's nearly noon when Julie wakes up. The pub is closed on Sundays and Julie has the day off. Blue sleeps on the pillow beside her. The sun stretches into the room from behind the curtains, defiant fingers reaching for the posters on the wall.

Julie pads to the bathroom. She runs the water while she pees, self-conscious of Blue overhearing. Confidence diminishes with daylight and sobriety. She brushes her teeth, too, scrubs the taste of last night's alcohol off the back of her tongue.

In the kitchen, Julie makes a pot of coffee. There is bread and cheese in the fridge for sandwiches. She heats the cast iron pan for frying. Blue appears when the coffee is ready. "Smells good," he says. He comes up behind her, his arms wrapping around her waist. Something melts deep within Julie's body, dropping between her legs. Her self-consciousness wanes. He's a nice guy: What is she so worried about?

Julie pours out two cups of coffee. She drops buttered bread into the hot pan. The slices sizzle. The cheese melts. The smell makes their stomachs growl. Blue sits on a stool at the kitchen counter. He points to a spot on the floor: "Look."

There, a black stain on the carpet, a dark circle not unlike a snake eating its tail. Just like the one Julie made on her white sheet, only smaller. Just wide enough to stand in if your feet were close together. "Was that there before?" Blue asks.

Julie stares. "I don't think so," she says. "We didn't spill anything last night, did we?"

"It's too perfect a circle for a spill," Blue says.

The bread starts to burn. Julie turns off the stove top, lifts the sandwiches onto plates, hoping Blue doesn't mind that one side is darker than the other.

"He was here," Blue says. "He must have been."

"Our ritual worked?" Julie asks.

"Maybe."

"How do we know for sure?"

Blue looks out the window, then back at Julie. "I know someone who can tell us if it was Matter. We can go see them today."

Jenny and Dorian have never spent a night apart. Ever since their parents brought them home from the hospital they've shared everything, including a bed. When they were six, their parents surprised them with their very own twin beds, each with tall, lace canopies. "Beautiful beds for beautiful little girls," their mother beamed.

But when Jenny and Dorian realized they would be

sleeping separately, they wailed and clung to the old, small bed they'd been sharing. They didn't know that it had taken their parents two years to save for their new beds. Not that they would have cared. Nothing would come between Jenny and Dorian. They cried and cried, and when their father pried their tiny fingers from the mattress so he could haul it to the curb, they kicked and screamed and threw their fists to the floor. Later that night, after their mother thought she had gotten them to fall asleep, Jenny and Dorian pulled all of their blankets and pillows onto the floor and slept together like they always did, curled up face to face.

Eventually, their parents gave in and pushed the twins' beds together so that "all that hard-earned money wouldn't go to waste."

As the girls got a bit older, they didn't care for their mother's tastes of antique lace and ruffled bed skirts anymore. They covered the pale pink walls with pictures they found in magazines of women they wished they looked like, always dark-haired models with red, wet lips. One day, when their parents were out shopping, they stripped the lace canopies from their beds and dyed them black in the washing tubs downstairs so that their rooms dripped with things dark and worn. When Jenny found a red silk scarf someone had lost at the bus stop one day, she brought it home to drape over the bedroom lampshade, casting the room in a crimson wave.

At night, Jenny and Dorian would lie in bed, waiting for the clock to strike midnight. Their parents were always asleep by then so they had to be quiet as they got out of bed to light the candles on their dresser. They would both somehow squeeze onto the narrow vanity bench and each place two fingers on the mirror whispering, "Bloody Mary, Bloody Mary" a hundred times over and then a hundred times again. Not because they thought she would appear, but because they had read somewhere that if you paid tribute to Bloody Mary, she would grant you with love and beauty for all eternity, an immortal queen, amen.

Other nights, Jenny and Dorian would sneak out and go to the all-night coffee shop where older boys would sit and smoke cigarettes and talk about books and bands and movies that Jenny and Dorian had never heard of before. Sometimes, their new friends would sneak them off to some clubs where people wore leather jackets and torn jeans and the music sounded like it came from a graveyard. "Baby faces, girls. You've got baby faces—should you even be here?" the bouncers would joke, but they would always let the twins in. After all, Jenny and Dorian were growing into young women and it took little for them to get noticed. Especially with the artful way they tore their black stockings and the deep, dramatic shades they painted their eyes. In the dank club light, it was easy to look older, and there was always someone willing to buy them cheap red wine so that they could watch the girls dance. Jenny and Dorian acted as though they were at the prom, always holding each other close and tight and going around in slow, lazy circles across the dance floor.

In those clubs where the city's strangest gather, they got the education of Starling City. For it's in those places—the dark, damp, basement venues—that the magic and wisdom of this place gets spilled. People carve the spells of the streets into the tabletops, everything a living grimoire. And after a few drinks, many tell of their saddest, scariest stories. The ones that still keep them up at night, the ones that are still so vivid that you get a shiver when you hear them.

That's how Dorian and Jenny learned some of their favourite invocations. One of the first they found true went like this: Go to the crossroads in the north end of town. Spit three times and turn counter clockwise. As you do, wish for a dark goddess to appear to you. Call her name, Hekate, and she will be there by your side.

Yes, these twins are the sisters who hail and welcome the words of a witch mother, amen.

That's also where Dorian and Jenny learned of city spirits whose names should not be spoken, though some people have forgotten that rule. Lucky for these girls, they forgot most of those names, too, thanks to the cheap red wine they loved so dearly. But if they knew what to look for they would find each of those names written on the bathroom walls, too.

But they remembered one name in particular: Matter. Some people said it was the name of a god, others a demon. Not that Jenny and Dorian were too concerned either way, because they both felt the same thing when that name was spoken: The sharp pull of pointed teeth running down the sides of their necks, the cold rush of strong hands down their arms, the tug of moisture behind their panties that nothing but their own hands had caused before.

Matter. His name is Matter, and Jenny and Dorian

devoted themselves to learning His story. They taught themselves how to read the stories of the streets in ways that one else could, deriving meaning from a splay of bottle caps, telling the weather by the way the crows cawed on Monday mornings. The girls collected things they found on the sidewalks—beads and coins, twigs and dogs' nails, the head of a broken doll. They put everything they found into a black velvet pouch and learned how to make these charms speak.

It's not the only thing they know how to read: They can throw down cards of any kind—poker cards, tarot cards—and tell you what they see. They speak to all kinds of spirits and know things about Starling City that are so arcane they have to be divined.

That's how they learned the names of gods even older than Matter. Names that people were made to forget long ago. But old gods don't ever really die; they just wait to be remembered. Jenny and Dorian took those names home, wrote them on their own walls, along the ceiling, spilling them down the bedposts. At night, they would close their eyes and recite this and other strange poems they wrote, things that rhymed and wept and crept into little spells.

Eventually, their mother stopped entering the twins' room altogether. She was afraid of what she'd seen in there once—an old woman crawling across the ceiling, staring down at her, something that Jenny and Dorian had woven out of their words though it wasn't the spirit they were hoping to summon.

Their mother had also become afraid of the miles of black gauze and torn lace that now filled the room. She didn't like the posters the girls had hung on their walls, or the words they had written on their dresser mirror. She didn't like the devilish faces Jenny had so beautifully drawn over the old pink paint, or the dark brown stains on the carpeting that she had never had the guts to ask about.

And when Jenny and Dorian's eighteenth birthday came around and the girls said they had found a little apartment downtown and were moving out, their mother burst into tears as many mothers do when their babies leave the home. But these tears were born of an unfortunate realization: This mother was relieved to see her girls go, because she knew they had brought something into that room that should never have existed.

Now, Jenny and Dorian are the oracles of Starling City. No one dares tell them they are wrong because they never are.

They leave witch bottles around town, the ones full of screams that Blue likes to collect. That's how Blue came to know them: He knew their individual breaths, the weight and density and differences between each of their lungs. (Did you know that the words you speak change the composition of the air you breathe out?)

Jenny and Dorian sleep next to each other every night. Their studio apartment is small and they like it that way. Their bed is tucked into one corner, the TV in another. There's a big, floppy chair by the window, a red velvet relic they dragged home from the Salvation Army. The kitchen is small, but they don't care much about that. They try to eat as little as possible, want to believe they can live on air alone.

When they can't, though, they drink coffee and smoke cigarettes and snack on bites of chocolate and sweets. Sometimes, when they can afford it, they go to a restaurant and share a tomato sandwich and a milkshake, or a plate of fries. They always sit in a booth by the window, side by side rather than across from each other.

Jenny and Dorian are in their apartment, sitting cross-legged on the floor picking at boxes of Chinese takeout. Greg, the older guy down the hall, dropped it off for them. "I worry about you girls. I never see you bringing in any groceries. No wonder you're such skinny things."

Jenny opens a box of rice, takes a few grains between her fingers, drops them on her tongue like pills.

"Do you think Blue has a crush on us?" she asks her sister.

Dorian chews at a spring roll. She cocks her head, thinking. She talks around the food still in her mouth: "Why wouldn't he?"

"I guess so," Jenny says. "He's kind of cute."

"And kind of weird," Dorian says. "You can have him, if you want."

"Wouldn't *that* be weird, though? I mean, it might be nice to date someone, or something. But then what would you do?"

"Maybe I could date someone, too. Or at least find someone to kiss."

"Kissing's easy. Let's find someone to kiss tonight," Jenny says.

Dorian smiles, nods. "Yum. The Spider's open. There's a band playing."

"Why wait?" Jenny asks as she leans over the takeout boxes and slides her tongue into her sister's mouth, tasting the grease off of Dorian's lips.

Speak of the devil: There's a knock at the door and it's Blue. Julie hangs behind him, shy again. She watches over his shoulder as Dorian opens the door. "Come in," she says. "Grace the hand with silver." She holds out her palm and Blue places a five-dollar bill there. "Thank you," Dorian says as she shuts the door behind them.

"What can we do for you?" Jenny asks. She lights a stick of incense to dispel the smell of green peppers and fried rice that hangs in the air. They all kneel on the small rug, which is covered in lint and long, loose hairs. Jenny lights a cigarette, offers one to Julie, who gratefully accepts.

"We think we summoned something," Blue says. "We think *He* came."

"He who?" Dorian asks.

Blue looks around and then lowers his voice as though telling a secret. "Matter," he says. "Can you tell us if it really happened?"

Dorian laughs and rolls her eyes. "Honey, He's always here," she says. "He's everywhere. He touches everything."

Jenny jumps in: "What I think you're asking," she says, "is did He come when you called?"

Dorian reaches for the black velvet pouch on their nightstand and shakes it all up. "Let us see," she says, arching an eyebrow and squinting through the curling smoke that surrounds the room.

"Pull," she says, holding the bag out to her sister.

Jenny closes her eyes, takes a handful of charms and throws them on the floor. They both lean down, looking for patterns and shapes.

"Do you see anything in there?" Julie asks, but the girls shush her quick. Julie blushes, part from embarrassment, part from jealousy. She wishes she could be the one to divine the unseen, and the one Blue could consult instead.

She also wishes she could excuse herself to the washroom, just to take a breath, but the apartment is so small that the bathroom is a shared suite down the hall. But then Blue reaches for her hand and holds it tight, and she lets herself focus on how perfectly their fingers fit together.

The twins start to speak: "I see Him here. Do you?"

"I do."

"He's coming. No. He's here."

"But where?" Blue asks, curious now. He tries to keep a straight face, but it's hard. What a legend he'll be for pulling off a summoning like this.

On the floor, the sticks and charms twitch. Alive and writhing, the divination has its own plans: "Soon, soon," Dorian says. "He will come back soon."

"How? Where?" Blue asks. Dorian shakes her head as though she's shaking something out of her hair:

"He doesn't come without a sacrifice. But then what does? The old gods know, better than anyone, that blessings must be given if they are to be received. That's why these gods are such fragments now. Filaments wailing through thinning forests, waiting for their congregates to return. To build them altars once again. To fill cups of wine and milk and blood and spill them into the earth where they will get lapped up like cats to cream. Too often now people forget about the old ones. They are not used to feeding gods anymore, have confused worship for a vending machine, only give their faith if a prayer is answered first. Where is the exchange in that?"

Jenny takes up a pen and paper, draws a map and writes out some instructions. The map leads into the woods. The instructions are a reminder that it takes so little to revive the lost ones: A candle burning for thirty consecutive nights. A name kept close to your lips at all times. Small offerings of hair or nail clippings at the base of a tree, or the opening of a path.

Dorian looks up from the charms, breaking her trance. Her eyes go from Blue to Julie. "Come here," she says to both of them, opening her arms. "Close your eyes. Call upon a name you know and tell me you can't feel something change in the air."

Blue and Julie close their eyes and rest their heads against Dorian's small, bony shoulders. She leans down between their heads, her breath in each of their ears: "In an old house in the woods, a girl sleeps beneath the floor. Buried there for years, her body remains intact, kept waiting. Go to her."

The season of the witch has begun.

9
The Body of the Moon

There are stories in Starling City that tell of street corners where people just disappear. They step off one curb and onto another and poof, they're gone.

Some stories say that the ones who go missing are lost to the stains where spilled wine has become a sacrifice and small portals remain for hungry ghosts or lost souls to step through and feed from the living.

Others say that the ones who go missing are still out there, walking the streets at night, but different from they were before—that they've met the true vampires of Starling City and were lucky enough to have been changed. There are rumours those ones live in an abandoned tunnel beneath the bus station.

There's another story that says the ones who go missing just ran into trouble in a bad neighbourhood, that they were out at the wrong time and on the wrong night and were too naïve to know what to do when they got into a jam.

And then there's the story that says one of the girls who went missing was killed and buried in the basement of an old house out in the woods. The house itself is as old as the city, the building itself a shell, all broken windows and a blackened fireplace. Anyone who's dared to live there hasn't lasted long, though only the very desperate have tried. The stories alone about that place have been enough to keep most locals away from it. Some say that the house isn't there at all: a phantom unto itself. But that seems an unlikely theory. There have been too many people who've walked through the woods at night and come out claiming they'd seen lights in the old home, heard voices flowing from its doorstep.

Either way, there's something wrong with the ground it's built on. Something wrong with the roots of the trees that grow around the building. They say that there's an underground river below Starling City that should run straight beneath that house, except you won't find any water there, but rivers of blood instead.

And in the basement of that house is a dirt floor, and that's where one missing girl has slept all this time. Aldea, her name was. Or is.

No one can say for sure how long Aldea went missing because her story has been around long enough now to become convoluted with details that don't matter much anymore. Some say she was a runaway from another town over, others aren't even sure if she ever existed. Maybe she was just a dream the city had while it slept one night.

The story that seems most important about Aldea is that some people say that she's not dead, only waiting. And that she knows the way to Matter. There's a story that says she slept under the earth for a long, long time, until Matter's own spirit walked over top of her and caused her to rise. Yes, vampires are more than bloodsuckers. Did you know that?

Do you believe it? Do you dare to?

It doesn't matter, really. Because there are enough people out there already who will give energy to fantasy until it is breathed to life. People say they've seen Aldea for themselves, been close enough to know the colour of her skin, teeth, hair. Two guys who hang out at the Lair once bragged that they had reached out and touched her, and that she had laughed and laughed with a voice full of dirt. That wasn't all that was wrong, though they were so surprised it took them a while to figure out what else was off about her: Nothing of her smiled, as though the sound of her laugh came from somewhere else.

If you ask Aldea herself, she'll tell you she's the one who collects all the prayers and whispers, wishes and offerings that all the kids send out into the night. All the right sounds find her as she rests within the earth beneath a dark house in the middle of the woods. She builds the sounds of strange voices into her body. She washes her hair with the perfume of intention. She holds it all to herself so that if and when she ever gets back to the heart of the city, she will feel familiar and warm to all of those who are looking to find their way to Him.

And it won't be long before she goes out to call them home. When the moon is right and certain planets align to swirl and bend and dance themselves into a talisman in the sky, Aldea will rise and this will all begin again. Even the wind and trees feel it. At night, the entire forest leans into itself and whispers, "Soon, soon."

And what exactly is it that is returning?

There are cycles in Starling City that only the locals who've lived here long enough will know. They come around on odd-numbered years and at uneven intervals, but they always come.

Nothing ever really dies here. Especially not old gods, or cruelty, or prayer. There are lots of things here, lots of spirits that are speaking to us all the time. You just have to learn how to listen to them.

Every prayer or wish or spell that gets sent out into the night sticks inside the city walls. It reverberates endlessly, becomes a spirit unto itself, though some spells are smaller spirits than others.

Those who know the cycles of this land know that certain gods always rise again. For a time. Like the seasons, they come to reap what has been sown and this year, the ground is ripe.

Those who know, know to expect disappearances. They know not to file police reports or go out into the woods when the neighbourhood kids go missing, no matter how desperate a parent's plea may be. Because there are seasons that exist only within Starling City, and sometimes they are seasons of death.

The ones who remember know to look the other way, trusting that the cycle that is coming will ebb and flow like it always does.

And of course, there are the ones who are willing the season to thrive.

Blue and Julie take the bus that stops at McCaffery Park. There, you can follow a trail that leads you into the woods that grow around the city. The same woods that Julie looks out on from her laundry room window.

Blue fidgets with the pockets of his army pants. He likes to keep things in the deep pouches and likes it even more when he forgets what's in there. Today, he finds a small surprise: two pills that have tucked themselves deep into the seams. He offers one to Julie and pops the other into his mouth. The pills dissolve before either can be swallowed. The bitterness seeps between teeth. The sun shines clean through the window.

Melt.

The pills make the ride feel fast. So do the kisses that Blue and Julie play upon each other's mouths. People stare, but that only encourages Blue to press his lips harder upon Julie's. He lets his mouth trail across her neck, and up behind her ears. She shivers and giggles at the wetness of his tongue.

When they get to the park, Blue and Julie take each other's hands and skip along the trail: La-la-la-la-la-la!

The map Dorian and Jenny drew for them is folded in Julie's bag. The lines made sense at the time, in the little apartment, but now look like a drawing of sticks and triangles. The yellow pills fizz and bubble through their veins. Blue bounces on the balls of his feet. "I think we should just let the woods tell us the way."

Julie lays the map down over the roots of an old tree: "Show us the way. We will have trust."

They walk until the path forks and choose to go left.

"What if we get lost? Or can't find it?" Julie asks as they come to another fork and again choose left.

But there's an arrow in their hearts that keeps pointing this way, that way, this way. They listen. And besides, as Blue says: "What difference does it make? I like wasting time with you."

The sun is perilously west when the black edges of a decaying roof peek through the treetops. Neither Julie nor Blue wear a watch but it feels like it's been hours since they got off the bus. Do these woods eat time, or accelerate it? It will be dark in another couple hours. Neither has bothered to remember the paths they've taken.

Still, here is the house. As described by Jenny and Dorian: dark and small, with broken windows. Inside, people have painted all over the walls: A green dragon with a red eye that seems to wink in the late afternoon light, litanies of chalk-white words and letters trailing around the doorframes.

Julie and Blue stand at the top of the stairs leading to the basement. The darkness below is velvet-thick. Blue pulls open a drawer in the kitchen and finds a white candle. Yet, even a single flame threatens to be eaten by the night that lives downstairs.

There's a story in Starling City that says if you knock on the ground three times, you will wake the underworld and whatever spirit may be buried below must answer. At the bottom of the staircase, Julie kneels down and knocks: One. Two. Three. Julie wants to believe that she knows this spell well, because she has tried it before on King Street. To invite the dead to dance. But if any spirits took her up on the offer, she never could tell.

Now, Julie and Blue wait, staring into the depth of shadow ahead of them. The basement is small, more like a cellar. There is a single small window high on the wall, obscured with dust and cobwebs. Blue wipes it away. Outside, tall grasses lean against the glass. Still, a faint light reaches in, the last dregs of another day. He looks around for a shape of some kind: a shallow grave, a burial mound. A hand reaching out from the earth.

"How long should we wait?" Blue asks. Half of him is nervous. The other half is skeptical that anything will happen at all.

"Let's give it a few minutes, at least," Julie says. She sits down on the steps and lights a cigarette. The smoke curls toward the soft light of the window.

The girl beneath the earth has been dreaming for a very long time. Often, she dreams of the soft body of the moon, which has arms that only she can see. Usually, the moon holds her. Its limbs are long and cold and she presses herself against it and the moon answers by telling her, over and over, that her name is Aldea.

The moon, of course, is a man. Or what used to be. The moon is a spirit, a memory. A moment in time. A disguise for something with a different name: Matter.

There is no warmth in the moon's arms, but that doesn't mean there is no tenderness. Aldea reaches for the moon, and the moon reaches back.

But today, Aldea's dream changes. There's a knock on the door that disrupts her sleep. A knock on the door that she barely remembers how to answer. Aldea tries to stay still, comfortable in a lunar embrace. Except the moon is slipping from her arms. Aldea reaches again but her hands grab onto nothing. No, her hands meet the earth, and they are digging. But in what direction? When you're underground, it's hard to know which way is up or down or sideways anymore.

But then there is light. Barely perceptible to most, but to Aldea, who's been asleep for so long, the gray gauze of twilight and dust is a neon dream. Above her, the sky leaks through a broken window, revealing the beams of the ceiling, the thick cobwebs that coat the corners of the basement.

Then the moon is gone, but Aldea is not alone. There's a spectre in the room, a memory so heavy she can feel the cloth of its old jacket against her face. She can smell the musk of earth, musty and wet, mixed with decades' worth of incense smoke and tobacco, the burnt offerings of hungry prayers to Matter.

Yes, He hears them all, collects every one. They keep His spirit alive.

There's another scent, too, so faint but there: the smell of flesh, decayed youth. Death sinking into blood and bone, the slow rot of aging.

Someone else is here.

10
Communion

It is just like something from the movies. The ground shifts. The hand reaching upwards is not quite so dramatic as it is in cemetery scenes where the dead rise, but it still happens. Just slower: The emergence of the edge of knuckle and fingernail, the plane of skin breaking ground.

The pills Blue and Julie took earlier are keeping the edges of fear soft and fuzzy. Adrenaline is fighting to break through, but is blocked by minds and bodies too mellow for more of a reaction than awe and nervousness.

While Blue holds his breath, Julie breathes in, then bites her tongue as her jaw clenches tight. Neither wants to break form in case this is magic, too, reliant on an unbroken focus and unwavering belief.

But as one hand digs itself out, and then another, it becomes harder to write off as hallucination. Julie doesn't notice that, as she grips Blue's hand, her nails are digging in tight, imprinting a trail of half-moons.

Blue is trying to swallow, but it takes effort, as though his throat wants to scream even though his mind is saying, "This is it, this is it: Something is happening." It is the first of many moments that will make Blue and Julie mythic in their own right: This is how stories in Starling City are made.

Now there are elbows, arms, shoulders, a head all clear out of the earth. Blue and Julie see a silhouette of a girl with a straight nose and long hair. Her thin torso breaks free of the earth. She pulls her hips and legs out next, long limbs, bone thin.

Aldea shakes the dirt from her hair as she sits up straight. Once the soil has loosened from her tresses, Blue and Julie see her full face. She's around their age, with hair as white as an old woman's.

Julie opens her mouth to say something—she feels apologetic, worried they've disturbed something that should have been left alone.

But Aldea raises her hand as though requesting a pause. She already knows the questions that are waiting to be asked. "You found me," she says, then coughs a little, clearing dirt from her throat.

"Someone told us to come," Blue says. "We're looking for help."

"I know," Aldea says. "You're looking for the one whose name means all things real and whole. Right? Well, He has been here. I know Him. He fed from me. I've kept Him sustained. This is the proof." She takes a lock of her hair and holds it in her fingers. "See? He said he was hungry for colour. I gave him the gold on my head."

Aldea doesn't tell them the other sacrifice she gave: the silence of her mind, which has opened up so wide that she can hear every ghost in town if she wants to. She thinks of the trade-off: the arms that have held her all this time. Aldea stands, motions for Blue and Julie to do the same. "Come," she says. "It's been so long since I've seen any other rooms of this old house."

She walks upstairs. Dirt shakes out of Aldea's old jeans with every step. A flannel shirt hangs loose off her shoulders, oversized against her diminished frame.

They sit in the main room of the old house. The fireplace is black, dead.

"We came to learn what more we can give to Him," Blue says. "To Matter, to show that we believe." He adds this last part hesitantly, afraid to say His name aloud. The power of it feels more real now, carries a different charge.

"He's like religion to us," Julie says, and then wishes she hadn't. Her voice sounds small, young in the expanse of this empty room. Not as poised as Jenny and Dorian's, not as deep as Aldea's.

"I know nothing of religion," Aldea says. "And what you offer Matter is not for me to decide. He picks what He wants. At least that's what He did with me." She sighs, looks out through a broken window. "There was magic in this place once. I have slept here so long I know everything about this house. This is the first place He was called to. Was summoned here long ago. There are curse tablets buried all around outside. A witch used to live here and made a pact with Him to keep this place."

"What happened to the witch?"

"I don't know," Aldea says. "The witch is no ghost that I'm aware of here. Nothing haunts this place but me, now. And Matter stays here, but is not tied here. He is greater than that, and older. He answered a call to come, and He did, decided to stick around. But where He comes from, and where He sends His followers, I don't know."

"Did you follow Him before this?" Julie asks.

"No," Aldea says. "He adopted me, left me here. I died here. He found me, held me in place. I gave Him what was left of me. But I know He's hungry. He's always hungry."

"Will you help us raise Him?" Blue asks. "We want to meet Him. Show Him what He means to us. He already came to us, once. We think. But He didn't stay."

"You want Him to change you," Aldea says.

"Yes," Blue says.

"I want that, too. For myself. Then I could live again. Look at me already: I should be rot by now, but the flesh stays on my bones. This is His magic, and the power that has been put into this place, this house. It's strong. I will help you if you help me. If He changes you, convince Him to change me, too."

"Of course," Julie says. The sun is nearly set now. The amber light fills the room.

"Take my hands," Aldea says, holding her palms out to Blue and Julie. They reach for each other, form a triangle. The meeting of three fates. Aldea's hands feel as evasive as a spider's web.

Aldea closes her eyes and says, "I am going to speak words that you need to remember. I am going to put them in your head and in your heart. Hold on to them, okay?"

She hums, rocking softly. Her voice builds to a strand of words, a delicate pattern of syllables that sound like a song played backwards.

When she's finished, Aldea lets go of their hands to signal the spell has been broken. The sun is stuck in the sky: It feels like hours have passed and yet the last dregs of daylight remain. Aldea looks down at her clothes, the clothes they buried her in. And her skin, dusty with dirt. "Remind me," she says. "There is a river near here, right?"

Blue and Julie nod in tandem.

"Take me there," Aldea says.

The forest stops singing when Aldea walks along the path with Blue and Julie. The animals don't want to make a sound so they play dead, knowing how easily they can be offered up on altars if they make themselves known. Only the trees shake and shimmer, unsure of whether dead girls are so reliable. They have seen this kind of thing before.

How many seasons do trees live through? How many cycles do they record in their rings? What do they tell each other when their roots meet deep beneath the earth? We think they are wise, but what if they are always laughing at us?

"Do I look familiar to you?" Aldea asks as they walk. Blue and Julie shake their heads.

"No," they say, but there are always so many dead girls to keep track of. When people in Starling City go missing, their bodies are rarely recovered. "Like they vanished into thin air," people are always saying, and in a way, they're right, for it's the ghosts and gods that feed on them first.

Awake now, Aldea wonders about town. Thinks of what it would be like to get herself some new clothes. And to do things she used to do there. A brief memory flashes throughout her body. In it, she's dancing, laughing, arms raised above her head. She wears an outfit she picked out just for that moment, each item carefully chosen. And then another memory of a warm body against hers, the heat of someone else's kiss.

Underground, she never thought much about these things. But then, she never thought she would leave. Now, that is changing. *Maybe I could be a real girl again, one day,* she thinks. A wind picks up and the trees titter now, rubbing their branches together like eager hands. "Soon, soon," they say.

"You know," Aldea starts, "there's a story in Starling City that says when you wake the dead, you better bring a gift. To keep favour. Did you bring me anything today?"

Blue can feel Julie's eyes looking to him for an answer. Their hearts are sinking. "I'm sorry," Blue says. "We didn't know."

"For next time, then. Because if I'm going to be changed, too, I'll need some new clothes, don't you think?" she tugs at her shirt to emphasize its tears and stains.

"Next time, for sure," Julie says, and Blue agrees. Neither of them want to talk more about it, afraid that the smallest mistake will prove this is all a mirage.

The sun is finally lowering when they get to the river's edge, time unstuck now. The air is still cool, as it tends to be in spring in Starling City, but it's enough for Aldea, who doesn't rely on the warmth. She takes her clothes off, leaves them on a rock. They are coated in dirt and have hard patches where Aldea's blood dried into the fabric. Beneath the dark stains you can make out a plaid pattern on the flannel shirt, colours that used to be green and blue. Aldea's tank top is torn on one side. The jeans are torn, too, but that may have been the style at the time of her death.

Clouds cover the setting sun. The sky becomes an ambivalent eye. Down the way is a sign: Beware of undertow. Aldea knows this is something more than a current. That the undertow is an entity onto itself, and there is no telling when it may wake.

Today the river is quiet, deep. Blue and Julie watch as Aldea sinks into a dark part of the water. Her head swims beneath the surface and the river turns red in response. She floats back to the top, allows her body to flatten, drift like a board. Her pelvic bones jut like tiny islands from the water's surface. Off in the distance, a dog barks.

Aldea looks over at Blue and Julie and waves. "That's enough for today," she says. "But see me again soon."

It's not as late as it seems when they get back on the bus. Neither of them want to say goodbye yet. Julie suggests watching a movie at her apartment. Blue is relieved that she's not expecting to be invited over to his place.

When they get back, Julie heats a can of soup and tells Blue to pick out a movie. Most of them are horror films. Blue picks one about a girl who's bitten by a vampire in New York City and is left to fend for herself.

Julie rests her head on his shoulder as they watch. He can smell her hair. She turns to him sometimes and says, "kiss me," and he does, and it's hard to stop. But they do, especially when Julie pulls away and says, "Oh, you have to see this part—this kill scene is insane." And as their attention floats back to the movie again, they wonder aloud: "Can you taste death or disease in someone's blood? Like, could you tell if they were terminally ill or something?" Julie asks.

"Probably," Blue says. "Your instinct might tell you. Do you think it would matter, if someone was about to die?"

Julie shrugs. The screen flashes red and purple. A pale scream jumps out of the TV.

"What if you drank from someone truly powerful, like a witch?" Julie asks, thinking of Jenny and Dorian and the jealousy she felt towards them before. "Would you gain their powers?"

"There's a story about Starling City that says something like that. Can make you lose your mind if you're not careful, though."

"Too powerful, maybe?"

Blue nods. "Probably. Unless you really needed it for some reason." Blue turns his attention back to the movie for a moment, then asks: "Do you think people will be scared to let you taste them? What if they fight you off, or get away?"

Julie watches the screen as she thinks. "I'd hope to be seductive enough that it wouldn't matter. That way, everyone would want me."

There's a slight tap at the window that shudders in time with the word "matter." Something's listening.

"Is there anyone else you'd want to turn into a vampire, too?" Blue asks.

"I like the idea of being able to," Julie says, "but I'd have to think about it. Right now there's no one that comes to mind. But maybe some day. We could start a coven. Or a family. Chosen ones."

The screen flashes red again. Another victim dies.

"If we become vampires, should we change our names, or stay as we are?" Julie asks.

"I like you as you are," Blue says. Julie smiles at this and answers, "I like you, too."

Later that night, asleep in Julie's bed, Blue dreams of a white-haired girl in the forest who holds a white rabbit in her arms. Around one of its legs is a band of red where she has reattached a severed paw.

"See?" She says. "Anything can be made whole again. You just have to know how."

As she speaks, her lips turn thin and black, stretching too far around her face. The lips of a dog. Blue wants to lean in to kiss them, but he can't reach her. In dreamtime, everything is always slower and farther than he wants it to be.

"We are on the level of the gods," the girl says. "Once you've seen us, you can't look away."

11
Polaroid Void

On Mondays, Blue seldom has anything to do. If he's lucky, he'll have money left over from the weekend. Sometimes he buys himself a plate of fries and a Coke at the diner. Usually, he just hangs out and waits for something to happen.

The problem is, not much happens around here on Mondays, so there isn't anything to wait *for*. The clubs are all closed and so are the old bookstores where Blue likes to hang out. Today differs from other Mondays, though. Today Blue is with Julie, waking up in her bed. Julie has work today, but that's okay. She will let Blue stay here if he wants. He can watch TV and wait for her to come home.

Julie's alarm clock is going off again. She has already hit snooze twice, lingering to cuddle against Blue. She doesn't want to get up, but forces herself to. She can't afford to be late for work again. Julie skips the shower and dabs baby powder into her hair to soak up some of the grease. She will twist it all into a messy bun and hope for the best. She washes her face and puts on fresh eyeliner, studying the pale purple shadows under her eyes.

In the kitchen she makes coffee and toast, choking both of them down. She kisses Blue on the cheek and says, "Wait for me to come back."

Blue stays in bed until noon. He doesn't sleep, just drifts on birdsong and sunlight and traffic sounds, the lulls of city life.

When he gets up, he turns on the TV to Sally Jessy Raphael: "I used to be a freak. Now I'm chic!" the headline screams. Blue rolls his eyes: Why would anyone want to stop being a freak?

At commercial he goes to the kitchen, finds a box of cereal and a giant bowl that holds half the box. He eats with a wooden spoon, milk dripping down his chin.

At one o'clock the TV is all infomercials and soap operas. Blue changes the channel to a station with no reception, turns up the volume on the static. He lights a candle on the coffee table.

There are so many spirits crying for attention in Starling City. Blue stares from the candle flame to the TV screen, which dances with black and gray snow. The anger of an image that can't be received. Blue turns up the volume on the TV as far as it can go and then speaks over it, inviting in whatever is waiting to be asked.

Blue smokes a cigarette. Waits. He lights a second smoke, lets it sit in the ashtray. An offering, to further entice a spirit. He listens for a rhythm in the static, breathes in time with a ragged thread he follows through the noise. He thinks of the city in all its directions, and then thinks of Aldea and the deal they made: If Matter comes, He will change her, too.

Blue wonders what it will be like when his body is not what he knows it as now: Will Blue remember how he was before this? Will he remember where things used to be, the spells he cast at every street corner? Or will becoming a vampire, something that was once alive, make him lose something of himself?

He listens to the static, allowing his mind to be led by it until his head is so full of voices it's hard to know which one to listen to. Finally, words cut clearly through the rest. The TV snaps off by itself. A ghost leans against it, arms crossed over its chest, staring down at Blue. "You think this will be any better when He comes?" the ghost asks. The ghost used to be a man. It's dressed in a light brown suit with a felt hat tipped over one eye.

"You think you're the first one who's done this? The first one who's called to Him? We've seen this all before, boy." The sunlight stretches through the window, brightening the room. The ghost pales, disappears.

Blue has finished his cigarette but the other still burns in the ashtray. Blue finishes it off. When he's done, he decides to shower. Before he goes into the bathroom, he turns back toward the living room, hoping to catch a final glimpse of his visitor, but it's too late. The ghost is gone, given Blue all he had to offer.

Julie comes home with a bag full of takeout containers from the pub: Fish and chips and coleslaw, baked potatoes,

English muffins. Blue heats it all up in the oven while Julie showers. When she comes out, she is wearing a black and red robe that Blue can see through when she passes by the window. Her hair is still wet. She picks at a piece of fish, her nails separating the flesh from the batter. She eats with her hands until her fingers are so greasy they, too, look wet.

Outside, Blue and Julie head towards the busiest streets. They look for pockets of people. They reason that if Matter is here, He will be where everyone else is. To blend in, to feed.

"Do vampires live off energy as much as blood?" Julie asks.

"I have a book that says they do," Blue says. "And on Sally Jessy once I saw someone talking about being a psychic vampire. They don't drink blood at all."

"That sounds so boring, though," Julie says. "Isn't blood part of the whole point?"

Blue and Julie both think of their own scabs and scars, the times they tasted and tested, pressing blades and pins to their skin, willing for it to break. Just to try. Just to see what it would be like.

There is a liquor store at the corner that sells bottles for cheap. Julie comes out with red wine and her and Blue sit on a stoop three doors down, the steps to a storefront long condemned. They list the true names of deities each of them knows to be tied to Starling City. (Did you know that some names we know old gods to have are just nicknames? It's true: Some of them are called only by sounds, vowels that modern tongues can barely pronounce.)

A neon sign flashes across the street. The red and orange lights are pale in the loitering daylight, fighting for attention. Still, the colours bounce, attract the eye. Red: Blue leans in for a kiss. Orange: Julie breathes, takes a drink of wine. Red: It's Julie's turn to kiss now. Orange: Another sip as a car speeds by.

What do we open ourselves up to when we sit in doorways and archways? Even thresholds that are no longer in use still retain their original purpose, don't they? Here, in the late afternoon sun, Blue and Julie open doors to blood and thunder, epiphanies to the seven sounds of creation.

When the bottle is done, Julie has to pee. "There's a 7-11 down the street," Blue says. The wind is picking up, carrying paper-thin prayers from behind brick walls. A lost five-dollar bill blows down the sidewalk. Blue catches it and stuffs it into his pocket. "Slurpees are on me," he says.

Blue waits outside while Julie pees. He looks at the missing persons posters that face out from the store window. There are so many that some of them overlap one another. He reads the names out loud. But then a face dislodges something deep within his throat, interrupting the litany. The picture is faded, and another poster covers the name, but Blue knows who it is: Aldea. In her photo, she's smiling at the camera. Her blonde hair hangs against a summer dress.

Blue coughs a little at this, moves on to the next name he can see: Brooke. He reads them all, out loud, louder every time. And with each syllable, Blue coughs again. Pebbles sputter from between his lips. He reads more names, and coughs, dirt dislodging itself from his esophagus. Mud rides up his throat. Larger clumps of earth rise from deep within Blue's body. When they hit the ground, they break open, showing that they are dry inside.

"Better not linger," a voice says from behind. It's another ghost, one that flickers on and off like a lightbulb about to burn out. "Sometimes the girls in those pictures get as hungry as I do. Boo!" Blue embarrasses himself by jumping. The ghost laughs.

There is a knock on the glass: Julie is inside, waving him in. Blue walks through the door. He is feeling the wine more than he expected. He follows Julie to the Slurpee machine, where she chooses all the red flavours. Later, as they share sips from the same straw, the red dyes will colour their lips and tongues and Blue and Julie will pretend they've been drinking something other than sugar and ice.

Outside again, Blue kicks at the clumps of dirt he coughed up, scattering patterns that fall into shapes of bugs and butterflies and fallen petals.

They walk without direction, eventually coming to the big department store next to the bus station. Here the buildings are tall and the sun doesn't touch the sidewalk, blocked by concrete heights. Blue and Julie like how people stare at them as they pass, taking in Blue's wild hair and Julie's haunted eyes. "I know what we should do," Julie says. "Let's get something for Aldea—the offering she wanted. Then we can go back again, properly this time."

"I don't have enough money," Blue says.

"You don't need any. I've got a big purse."

The fluorescent lights of the department store assault their eyes. It's not very busy, just a few women on their way home from the office who are browsing purses and pantyhose. Blue and Julie walk towards the back, where the shoes are. "What size do you think she is?" Julie asks.

"Your size, maybe," Blue says.

"She's taller than me, though. Let's try the next size up." Julie takes two black loafers off a table and drops them into her bag. Next they ride the escalator up to the second floor, where they find racks of jeans and t-shirts. Julie holds up tops and pants against her body. She stares at herself in the mirror, surprised at how tired she looks. She gets a flash of what she might look like as she gets older, Polaroid void. She shakes her head—no need to worry about that for long, hopefully.

Julie puts a pair of jeans and a t-shirt in her bag to follow the shoes. On their way back to the escalator they pass a table of shawls. Julie takes one of those, too. Aldea probably also needs a jacket, but it will be too hard to steal today. Do the dead even feel the cold?

Blue and Julie walk back outside. No one chases after them. Towards the bus station are more ghosts, the spirits of those who got lost when they came to this town, or died trying to get out. Some rub their hands together nervously when Blue and Julie walk by, knowing what they represent better than either of them can understand.

It's dark by the time they get to McCaffery Park. "Should we still go, or wait until tomorrow?" Julie asks.

"Things will happen faster if we make nice sooner," Blue

says. "You want this, right?"

Julie steps close to him. "So, so badly," she says, and then kisses Blue as though to emphasize her words.

On a path that, long ago, was built with dirt alone and used as a crossroads of promises and pacts, Blue closes his eyes and listens. He waits just long enough to hear what he needs: "This way, this way," the voices of Starling City seem to tell him. Blue enters the forest with Julie following close behind.

12
Offerings

There's a story in Starling City that says that the house where Aldea sleeps was built on sacrificial ground. Mothers and fathers used to bring their children here during hard winters—children who were already a breath away from death, who would not last the season. It was easier to give these up.

Someone has left an old sleeping bag in the corner of the main room. Half-burned candles rest along the mantel. Bottle caps and broken glass on the floor. But dust and old leaves cover everything. No one has partied here for a very long time.

The house is happy to have guests. When Blue and Julie break off the path and into the clearing, they hear voices even though they are alone: laughter or tears, it's hard to tell. The house groans, too, as though reshaping itself, stretching its bones to make space for guests. Or making space for the slippery frame of a question that can't be answered with language as we know it now.

Julie knocks on the earth: One, two, three. It doesn't take as long for Aldea to rise this time. She was expecting them, maybe. Or at least hoping they would return.

"We brought you something," Julie says, removing the clothes from her tote bag. She lays them out, folded and lined up. Blue runs upstairs to take candles off the mantle so Aldea can see her offerings.

"Show us what we're looking for," Blue says.

There's a story in Starling City that says Matter has taken many forms: That beautiful women and strong men have hosted Him in their bodies. That He has lived as an old crone and a young child. There is even a story that says that in at least one or two instances, Matter has even inhabited the bodies of black cats.

What determines the form a god will take when it returns to these streets? Some stories say it depends on the devotees and their dreams and imaginings of how the Divine may appear.

What do you imagine an old god would look like?

What appears behind your eyes when you shut them tight and call out a name that dares not be forgotten?

Other stories say that a god's form depends on its own preferences: That though gods can embody many forms, they are most likely to choose a proper host based on their own tastes, ideals and imaginings.

Those who honour the dreams of deities better their chances of effective workings.

There are a few stories that say Matter likes long hair and attractive eyes. That He likes tall bodies and wide shoulders. That He likes strength in the legs and hands because He alone has no force—it must be available in the form He inhabits. To build that strength once He arrives is difficult, so it's better if it's already established. Most of His energy and sustenance will go to keeping Him here once He resurrects. A corpse revived is still a corpse; fed with blood and life it can be maintained, but rarely changed.

"Show me the city," Aldea says. She looks Blue in the eye as she speaks. "Show me where there are people and I will show you the way I know to call Him."

Aldea undresses in front of them. She is wearing the same clothes they watched her strip from by the river. She pulls on the fresh jeans and clean t-shirt. Everything hangs loosely from her but she likes it all, rolls the jeans up at her ankles. Slips into the loafers, wiggles her toes. She runs her fingers through her long, white hair, which hangs in tangles down her back.

"You look perfect for where we're going," Julie says. "But not today. We can't take you today. It's not open."

Something moves across Aldea's face: a shadow of disappointment, maybe. "You will come back for me."

She says it more like a fact than a question. Blue and Julie look at each other. Tomorrow is Tuesday. Nothing worthwhile will happen until Thursday.

"In a couple of days," Blue says. "We can even bring more clothes. Or something else for you."

Aldea looks back and forth from Blue to Julie. "Bring me now. To stay with you. Just until I can show you what I can do, and then I will leave. Promise."

Aldea's head fills with voices as soon as they get out of the park and onto the streets. So many ghosts want to become gods. They tap at her shoulders and blow their cool breath into her hair. They whisper their names to her in the hopes she will remember them. They want to be seen and heard and felt. After all, what else is there to do in this town?

Aldea pushes away the noise that builds around her. The specters see her for what she is, the bridge she can be between the living and dead. But she can't let all of them cross with her. "Stop!" Aldea yells, fists clenched and teeth white behind her lips. A few people on the street stop, stare. All they see is a young woman with wild, white hair and drapes of dark clothing and they know enough to ignore her.

Starling City is full of people who are yelling at things no one else can see or hear.

Blue and Julie hold Aldea's hands until they get to Julie's apartment. Aldea's skin feels as dusty as the old books they flip through in the antique shops downtown.

Inside, Aldea looks at herself in Julie's mirror. She turns and twists, takes in her clothes, her hair.

"Do you want something to drink?" Julie asks.

Aldea shrugs at her reflection: "Sure."

Julie pulls down three glasses from the cupboard, takes a bottle of wine from the fridge. Aldea chokes on the first sip. Her body no longer needs to know how to swallow. The wine hits the carpet. It will leave a stain. Aldea does not apologize.

Blue passes a yellow pill to Julie before sliding one into his mouth as well. He turns on the TV and finds a movie to watch. Aldea looks around and says, "This is nice."

Julie and Blue are in bed when Aldea crawls in with them. They left her on the couch, under a blanket with her head resting on a throw pillow. The pills Blue and Julie took are heavy with the wine. Their bodies and heads can barely swim out of dreamtime.

Aldea kneels over top of them. Her long hair is in their faces. Her mouth is hanging open, letting out a long, low hiss.

Blue is the first to wake. "Let me give you another ritual," Aldea says. "This one was buried deep within me. So deep I didn't know it was there until I drank that wine. The choking freed something from me."

13
To Summon a Demon: Lesson 2

Access every memory the city has recorded. How? Here, like this:

Touch your hand to a tabletop at a bar. Close your eyes and feel the linoleum beneath your fingers. Or the whorls of wood: What do they tell you about the hands that have touched them before yours? Listen, listen: When people talk amongst themselves, where do you think their words go? You don't retain every single word ever spoken to you, do you? You don't hold on to those conversations letter by letter. All you take in is what you need to hear, or want to hear. Sometimes all you take in is the image of the moment itself. Sometimes the feeling of it. Sometimes, you remember nothing at all.

Right?

But the tabletops catch it all, because the words spill down like spilled drinks and there, you can find the memories of so much of what's been spoken here. Even words spoken when no one can hear each other, shouting through the loudest songs or busiest debates. Once a word is created, it lives on.

You can access all kinds of memories in this way. Look

at all the old chewing gum that's flattened on the sidewalk. Black portals into the DNA of someone's dreams, their oral secretions telling of every kiss that has taken place on these streets, every prayer that's been offered.

What might you learn if you were to crouch down and press your index finger to one of those black spots on the sidewalk? You won't know until you find out.

Think of all the spaces and places in the city that someone else has touched. People have died on the streets, you know. They have died in the apartments upstairs from your favourite stores and been born in the backseats of used cars.

Use your imagination as to what you can tap into. And when you're ready, let the city speak to you. Take all the words it offers. Write them down so you don't forget them—because you *will* forget them, I promise you that.

Once you've recorded your messages, cut them up and weave them into a spell. It doesn't matter the order: Whatever sounds right to you will become your summoning.

14
Imaginal Spaces

Julie has to go to work and doesn't want Aldea alone in her place all day. Blue has not been home in days and wants to make sure his mother knows he is still alive.

He takes Aldea home with him. It is a forty-minute walk from Julie's to Blue's. People stare at Aldea but they don't know why. There is something about the girl with the youthful face and long, white hair that confuses their vision. A puzzle they are not aware of trying to piece together.

At the corner of King and Barton they run into Jenny and Dorian, who eye Aldea, too. The girls have set up a small card table and have their legs tucked underneath folding chairs. There is a sign that says: Tarot Readings Five Dollars.

Blue reaches into his pocket for a bill but the cards are already turning themselves. Some of them leap out of the deck and go tumbling down the sidewalk, caught up in a wind no one else can feel. Jenny goes running after them. Dorian stays, transfixed on the cards that place themselves face up in front of her. When they are all visible, she shakes her head and spits twice. She glances at Aldea before speaking to Blue: "Be careful," she says.

The TV is on when Blue gets home. His mother is asleep

on the couch. There's something about the familiar smells of the apartment that make Blue realize how tired he is.

"Mom?" he whispers into the living room. No answer: She's passed out, an empty mickey of vodka on the floor beside her. Someone is snoring in his mom's bedroom. Blue peeks in and sees a man, shirtless with his jeans undone. Blue can't quite see his face but he doesn't seem familiar.

"I'll take you to my room," Blue says to Aldea. "You can hang out there."

Aldea goes to the candles on Blue's desk, lights them.

"Pretty," she says. She sits and hums, the tune of something mournful that slithers into Blue's ears and rests between his eyes. He stretches and takes off his shirt. "I'm gonna take a shower," he says. "You're welcome to use the bathroom or something, too, when I'm done. If you want."

But Aldea only nods and keeps staring at the candle flame.

In the shower, Blue crouches in the bathtub and lets the hot water run over him. There is a small window above the bathtub. A breeze is coming through. The light dances with the steam. Blue has always loved moments like this, when anything seems possible.

What will be possible if Blue becomes something else? He doesn't like to admit that if it turns out to be true, that vampires must avoid the sun, Blue will miss the light.

There are footsteps in the hall, and then the clatter of dishes in the kitchen. Glasses and plates tumble to the floor. His mother must be awake. Maybe her date, too. Blue hurries to dry off, wondering if he should tell his mother about

Aldea, or keep her a secret. Blue's mother does not like people over unless they are there for her.

There is a handprint on the wall, blood on the floor. A pair of feet stick out from his bedroom door. Blue runs with the towel held at his neck like a cape. The man that was in his mother's bed is now bleeding out on Blue's rug. Aldea has dragged him through the big ashtray on the floor and cigarette butts are stuck to his body, skin blackened with ash.

"He wanted it," Aldea says.

"Who?" Blue asks. "Who wanted what?"

Aldea's eyes widen. She cocks her head toward the candle. "Matter," she whispers, saying it as though Blue should already know this by now. "He's hungry. You want Him to show up, right? Well, He can't do that if you don't feed Him first."

Blue doesn't notice his bath towel has dropped around his feet. Blood is coming out of the man's ears. With a closer look, Blue knows for sure he doesn't recognize this man from the others his mother has brought home. He feels unexpectedly relieved by that, as though it's easier to watch a stranger die.

"What are we supposed to do with this guy?" Blue asks. It's normal for humans to panic at the sight of blood. An instinctive response. Blue tells himself to override it: *Get used to it*, he thinks. *Remember that this is what you want.*

A stream of blood runs off the man's cheek. Aldea dips her finger into it, tastes it. She looks at Blue. "Do you have a bowl?"

Blue checks under his bed, hoping to avoid going to the

kitchen. Luck is on his side: He finds a white plastic popcorn bowl he'd forgotten about under there. He hands it to Aldea, and she holds the man's head so his blood drains into it. Blue watches at how the red splatters against the sides of the bowl. He swallows, trying to push away the slight feeling of sickness that's coming on. He tries to think of what Matter might say if He were here:

Imagine it differently.

Imagine it becoming anything you want.

This is what I wanted to show you.

Now open your eyes again. Ask: What would a vampire do?

In the books Blue has read, some vampires steal their victims' wallets, surviving on the money they find or using the I.D.s if they can. He checks the man's pockets and pulls out a worn leather wallet, warm from the body heat that will soon fade. There is a license inside: Peter Mott, 47. There is also a picture of two children. The pictures look old, corners bent as though they've been carried around for a long time. Blue doesn't look at these for long. Can't.

There is more cash in the wallet than Blue thought there would be: a hundred and sixty bucks. He slides it into his own pocket, then drops the wallet on the floor rather than putting it back into Peter's jeans.

"There," Aldea says. The bowl is full to the brim. She sets it in front of the candle and bows. "Ritual complete."

"What do we do with the body?" Blue asks. The sounds of birds and cars from outside fill the beat of silence that follows the question. Blue can hear people talking as they pass by on the street.

Aldea looks around Blue's room. Her eyes settle on a large canvas bag Blue uses for laundry. "This will do," she says. She holds the bag open and tells Blue to help her get it over Peter's head and shoulders. Then she pulls the bag over the rest of him. The body, still warm and pliant, curls up inside like a doll. Blue picks up Peter's wallet, doesn't want to keep anything hanging around here just in case.

Aldea carries the bag over her shoulder like it's nothing. Like it is just a bag of laundry and her and Blue are off to wash their clothes. They leave it in a dumpster in the alleyway behind the pizza place two blocks down. Tomorrow is garbage day, and hopefully it will be long gone before anyone notices. If Peter is anything like Blue's mom, it won't be unusual for him to be gone all day or all night without a word.

At the bridge that crosses the river, Blue tosses the wallet into the water below. The current is fast today, the undertow willing and hungry. If his mother asks, Blue will tell her that Peter got up and left while she was asleep.

"Now what?" Aldea asks.

Blue fidgets with the money in his pocket. There's a bar three blocks from here, the Green Man. It will be quiet at this time. Blue takes Aldea there.

The Green Man is a dark bar with a sunken floor and red velvet booths. Marble inset in the walls, mahogany furniture. A relic from another time, maybe, when Starling City was something bigger, richer than what it is today.

Now the Green Man is a place where you can get a beer

couple of bucks or a glass of cheap red wine that will go straight to your head. The corners are dark and the poets sit here all day, drinking coffee refills and scribbling in their notebooks.

"You ever had one of these?" Blue asks. He holds up a yellow pill for Aldea. Both of them have ordered wine but Aldea can only taste hers. She takes tiny sips and then spits them back out into the glass.

"I don't think it will work for me the way it does for you," Aldea says. In the bar's shade she looks even younger, her hair wilder. She has let her shawl fall around her waist. Her long arms stick out at awkward angles. Blue has a sudden urge to kiss the soft crook of Aldea's arm. Would she let him?

A question forms in Blue's mind: When was the last time Aldea was kissed?

But Blue holds back. Forces himself to think of Julie.

He pops the pill in his mouth, washes it down with wine. He finishes half his glass in one go, pours more from the decanter they're sharing.

"If you want to try it," Blue says, holding the pill out to Aldea again, "it's yours. Just let me know."

She looks at the wall, then back to Blue. She takes another sip of her wine and, this time, manages to swallow. "Let me try something," she says, and she drops the pill into her glass where it dissolves. The wine will be bitter, now, strange medicine.

The music speeds up overhead. Blue's words do, too. He talks at Aldea about the things he has done: candles he has burned, their colours. He tells her of the spells that gave him what he wished for fastest and the ones that never worked.

He also tells her of a dream he has had since he was a kid: a dream about a tarot card that is not a tarot card, but a door. And if he says the right words, it will open and let him inside. Except that he can never remember the words to get back out, and when he realizes he's trapped is always the moment he wakes up.

He tells her, too, about his sister, Samantha. He asks: "Did you know her, maybe? She used to go to the woods, too." He pulls out a picture from his pocket and tries not to think about the pictures that were in Peter's wallet earlier.

"See? She had dark hair and eyes, like this. She was pretty, like you."

Aldea looks, taking the photo between her fingers so delicately that Blue almost cries. Aldea shakes her head. "No, not her. I didn't know her. But there are others, you know."

"Others?" Blue asks.

"In the woods. Some of them are ghosts, stuck there. Some have been buried there, like me. Who or what they obey, or whether anything greater keeps them there, I don't know. But sometimes, when I was under the ground, I could hear them."

"What would they say?"

"Some of them cry. No words, just sounds. Some of them ask for help. Others are mad and laugh about worms and rodents that dig against them. Some don't speak at all, just tap their fingers against the earth, trying to replicate the patterns of footsteps overhead. To let you know you're not alone out there."

"No one is ever alone in Starling City," Blue says.

He raises his glass and tells Aldea to do the same. They clink their wines together and drink. Blue orders more. The pills they've eaten are eating the time. The only windows are at the front of the room, casting long shadows throughout the rest of the bar. The nature of light and shade makes it easy to lose track of the day.

Aldea goes to the bathroom.

As soon she's out of sight, someone else is at Blue's shoulder. "May I speak with you for a second?" He expects it to be the server, but no: It's Samantha.

"Shit," Blue says. His sister's ghost slides in where Aldea was sitting. Sam dips a finger into Aldea's wine, brings it to her mouth for a taste.

"You shouldn't have woken her," Samantha says.

"But—"

"You shouldn't have brought her here, to the city."

"But—"

"You shouldn't have taken those spells from her."

"But, Sam, she's coming back," Blue says, seeing Aldea crossing the room. "You should go."

And his sister does, even though it pains Blue to ask her to leave.

Aldea lifts her hair off her shoulders, wipes at her shirt the way you might if it was covered in crumbs. "There are too many damn ghosts in here," she says. "They got all over me in the bathroom. Hungry, hungry, all of them."

Aldea picks up her wine again, no problem swallowing now. "I had more life left in me than I realized," she says, and clinks her glass against Blue's again.

It's on the walk back to Blue's apartment when they kiss. It happens on the bridge, in the same place Blue threw Peter's wallet into the river hours earlier. That memory is far from Blue's mind at the moment, distanced by wine and his mother's magic pills.

Aldea is looking up at a streetlight when it happens. She points her finger up in the air and says, "If you listen to the hum each light makes, you will hear the poetry of the city within it. It gets encoded in the electricity. You could sit here, if you wanted, with a notebook and become an artist."

It's her arms, her elbows that get him. He wraps his hands around Aldea's biceps and pins her arms to her sides, holding her softly in place. Aldea's lips feel like moth wings fluttering against Blue's mouth. He lets his tongue touch hers and finds it cold but receptive enough that it touches him back. With his eyes closed, something dances through his mind: an image of a little girl in a white dress spinning, spinning in a dark room.

15
The Ghoul House

Blue is still asleep when the phone rings. It's nearly two in the afternoon. His head swims as he opens his eyes. The light is creeping through the blinds, which are bent, haphazard in places. Blue has always hated how he can tell the time just by the sun's position, the passage of life inescapable. Dreaded.

Normally, Blue would let the phone go. Normally, his mother would yell at him by now not to answer it.

The apartment is quiet. She must be out.

Blue thinks of Julie. Ever since he met her, he's been finding her on his mind within moments of waking: The softness of her lips, the warmth of her body next to his.

And then the guilt hits him deep in the gut as last night's memories come flooding back. He hates how that happens, waking up after being blackout drunk and thinking in that first moment that everything is normal. And then, a breath later, remembering all the shit that happened the night before and realizing he can't go back and change it.

He remembers how Aldea's tongue felt like velvet, the kiss like turquoise. Aldea, who is asleep under Blue's bed. Asleep in a dark place just like she would be if she were still in the woods.

Blue reminds himself that she'll only be here another day or two. Until Matter comes, finally. Which He will, right?

Right?

The phone is still ringing. Blue picks it up. "Hello?"

It's Crook. Blue rubs his face. The pressure behind his eyes is tight. A hangover rages deep within him, building momentum.

Blue met Crook a couple of years ago, when Crook was still new to the scene and ended up at Kevin Dyer's place one day. They never really became friends, but Crook calls Blue now and then to score some pills. He has a girlfriend named Cassie who Blue suspects is just a poser.

Blue thinks Crook is a creep, but he's always willing to take his money.

"Hey Aldea," Blue says as he hangs up the phone. "Do you want to go for a walk today?"

Cassie sits in the yard and watches the birds. She fidgets with the necklace that sits between her breasts, a crow's head that hangs from a silver chain. She found the skull in a cemetery last year. The meat had already fallen off the bird's bones, and most of its feathers had blown away. Cassie had plucked its skull between her fingers and said, "Mine."

Later that night, she had dreamt of an old woman who scolded her for separating the bird's body: "Now it will be bound to the earth, in search of itself and the memories it had. Don't you know that crows are not what they seem?"

Cassie had woken up laughing. "Silly old woman," she had mumbled into the darkness before turning over and falling back to sleep.

A family of sparrows has built a nest in the oak tree that grows tall on the neighbour's lawn. Its branches reach over the fence towards the Ghoul House. The Ghoul House is where Cassie lives with her boyfriend, Crook, and an assortment of housemates that always seems to be changing, revolving to the point where no one bothers to keep up with who's coming or going anymore.

Cassie sits on the bare grass, brown and dry from where winter's fingers dug in. The neighbour's lawn is already coming in green. When the grass of the Ghoul House does finally grow in, it will be tall and patchy, unwatered and left to run wild.

Cassie pours birdseed into her hand and holds out her palm. She stays very still, so still as to be a statue, so still as to not scare the birds that flutter above her. The mother sparrow ducks into the yard and pecks at the earth. In seconds she rises again, a worm dangling from her beak. The baby birds scream. The nest quakes.

The sparrows eye Cassie wearily. They see what she is offering, but no matter how still she gets, these ones know better than to go near someone who wears the bones of another bird.

Cassie always comes out here to be with the birds after a bad night. And today will surely be more of the same. Blue will be here soon with a special order for Crook. Cassie asked her boyfriend not to call his drug dealer today, to give it a rest.

Other couples go out for breakfast or have coffee or sex in the morning. But it seems more often than not that Crook is hungover and so they never do anything. Like today, because he drank so much last night that he tried to fight the bartender. Later, he threw up on the sidewalk on the way home.

It's the third time Crook has gotten them kicked out of a bar this month. When Crook drinks, he forgets everything and everyone. He forgets where he is. He forgets his legs and his arms and his whole body sometimes. He forgets that it's not all about him. He forgets how many drinks he's already had that night and doesn't understand why he can't fit any more into his body. In the room that Crook and Cassie share, there are holes in the walls where Crook's fist has broken through when he has been upset over an imaginary grievance or perceived slight. The holes in the wall match the gap in Cassie's smile where her father once knocked out her eye tooth when she was younger.

Cassie learned early on not to try to calm Crook down on nights he had too much to drink, or tell him what to do, but instead to just put him to bed with a bucket on the floor. She had learned how to do all of these things because she had seen her mother do the same for her father. Cassie took her lessons gratefully. So far they had helped her to keep the love she had with Crook, and she was sure they would one day help save him from himself.

Today, though, Cassie is tired. Last night, after getting

home, she had brushed her teeth and washed the makeup off her face, then came into the room to find Crook passed out in bed, his whole body thick and wide and tall taking up every inch of their tiny twin mattress. Cassie had crawled over him, careful not to wake him though that would have been impossible, and pressed her body against the wall the mattress is shoved up against. She imagined herself flattening as she tried to take up as little space as possible, wishing she could become so small as to slip between the cracks of the baseboards, to become so tiny as to not need to be anywhere at all.

Cassie tries not to let anyone else in the house know that it gets to her. If she has to cry, she does it in the shower. Which is what she did this morning before getting dressed and coming outside to sit with the birds. Days like today when she doesn't have anywhere to go are the worst. Cassie only works part time and her next shift isn't for another two days. The time between now and then stretches ahead of her, feeling impossibly long.

She is starting to hate living here, but has nowhere else to go. Crook is not only her boyfriend, but her only friend, too. When she moved here, she had hoped she'd become closer to the other housemates. Especially the other girls. But everyone seems too busy for new friends. They all have inside jokes and routines with each other that keep Cassie on the outside.

Cassie once read a story about a girl who made friends with birds and discovered all their secrets. Cassie held onto this idea, wishing it could happen to her, too: That she could learn how to fly. And how to carry the prophecy of death. And understand the mystery captured beneath silver's reflection.

Her hand is getting tired of holding up bird seed. She sighs, looking up at the sparrows as though they should be grateful for the seeds she is offering. But they don't give in. Resigned, Cassie throws the seeds, which scatter across the yard. Within moments, the sparrows descend, as do other birds Cassie didn't even know were near. She reaches into the pocket of her hoodie and takes out a chicken bone that has long been dry and white, clean as a dinner plate, and begins to suck on it like a farmer chews at straw. She stands up and heads back inside.

After a quick, cold shower and three deep chugs from a tepid black coffee he buys at a corner store, Blue has made it to the Ghoul House. Aldea has come, too. Sensing that Blue was still getting his head together, Aldea didn't press for conversation on the way.

Blue knocks at the door, then lets himself in, as is the custom.

They call it the Ghoul House because to walk up to the front porch is to enter through the gaping jaws of a black cat, a haunted house relic that one of the housemates found at an antique market. One of the cat's fangs is missing, making it even more of an impressive eyesore.

Behind the cat's mouth is a dilapidated porch, collapsing

on one end where the weight of a flattened brown couch shoulders the effort of slack. It's dark back there, the light of day mostly blocked out by the huge haunted house panel. There are stubs of old candles and melted wax dried into the floorboards here. Empty beer cases are stacked at the other end, waiting to be returned for a refund. It's always a two-person job, taking back the empties, requiring one to pull the little red wagon that hauls the cases to the beer store up the street, and another to hold the bottles in place to make sure they don't slide off and break.

Inside, the house is just as dark as the porch. The living room curtains are always drawn and the lights are always off, save for the purple lava lamp. A thin scream curls up around Blue as the door closes behind him. It's coming from the movie Troy and Sandy are watching on the TV. The walls turn red as blood spatters across the screen. They are in their pajamas. "Hey," Troy says.

"Hey," Blue says back.

"Crook's upstairs," Sandy says. She barely looks away from the television screen.

Someone is always watching a movie or playing video games here, sinking deeper into the sofa with every hour that passes.

Most of the walls in the house have been painted black, or covered up completely with movie and music posters: Dracula and Danzig, Elvira and Bauhaus. There is always a stack of dishes in the kitchen sink and the mugs and wine glasses are all chipped. The oven is only used for making bags of frozen fries, or heating up cans of soup on winter days when coughs and sniffles run through the whole house.

Dustin's room is next to Crook's. Dustin's door is always closed, locked even when he's in there. Blue has sold some pills to him before, too, but only when there's a shortage of magic mushrooms in town. Otherwise, Dustin never seems to go out. You never see him at any clubs and even his housemates say he only comes into the kitchen at odd hours when everyone's asleep or out. You only know he's home because the sounds of Skinny Puppy grind their way out from under his door.

Dustin's music clashes with Led Zeppelin's *Physical Graffiti*, which is coming out of Crook's room. This is the album Crook plays whenever he is hungover. Sometimes Crook and Dustin can hear each other's music through the thin walls, and it leads each of them to crank theirs a little louder. No one ever wins this game. It gets so loud the neighbours complain sometimes, but only dare to yell their pleas from across the yard. They don't have the guts to knock on the door, or to call the cops.

Blue knocks on Crook's door. The movement makes his head throb, and he's grateful, as always, for the darkness of the house. Aldea hovers at his shoulder, like a feather floating through the air. "Come in," Cassie calls.

"Oh, hey," she says when the door pops open. "Crook's in the shower."

Cassie is stretched out across the bed, reading an old *Spin* magazine, the one with Trent Reznor on the cover that everyone has held onto. She is only wearing her loose black hoodie and a pair of underwear. Her face is wet and her wide, pale pink panties are loose around her bum. She's smoking a cigarette and the windows are open. Nag Champa incense smoulders on Crook's bookcase but there's a slight smell of vomit that's just strong enough to break through these layers. Cassie sees Aldea over Blue's shoulder and moves to pull the sheet up over her body. "You didn't tell me you were bringing anyone," she says. "I was just going to lay down for a minute."

"Sorry," Blue says. "This is Aldea. She's staying with me for a couple days."

Blue steps out of the way for the girls to see each other. "If he left any money with you, then I can leave these," Blue says, holding up the little baggie of goodies Crook ordered.

Cassie snorts. "Yeah right," she says. "You know how he is." She nods at the desk. "Sit down. He won't be that long." Blue takes a seat in the wooden chair. It's the kind that rolls and swivels and Blue tries to keep himself as still as possible so as not to send his head spinning again. He silently wills the coffee he drank earlier to start working faster.

Aldea hovers in the door, staring at Cassie. "Birds," Aldea says. "You know the birds."

"What?" Cassie asks. Her cigarette smoulders between her fingers. She takes a deep puff to hide the quiver that's starting to show in her hands.

"Your necklace, I mean," Aldea says. "I like it. I can show you some bird calls, if you'd like. I like birds, too."

Cassie's face softens, calms down. She looks around at the mess of the room, suddenly embarrassed. Crook's desk holds an overflowing ashtray and a stack of dirty plates. A pile of old magazines sits underneath. A sword hangs over the bed and the only curtain is a Misfits flag that's been faded by the sun. The carpet is stained and burned from cigarettes. There are yellow butts on the floor, getting mixed in with small piles of clothes of varying degrees of cleanliness. She doesn't want this girl to see this.

Maybe this girl could be her friend.

Cassie reaches behind the night stand for a bottle of white wine, pours it into a disposable cup. "Drink?" she asks. Aldea shakes her head no. Blue feels last night's wine rising in his throat and takes a pass, too. Cassie shrugs as she takes a big gulp, followed by a long drag of her cigarette. "Suit yourselves," she says, and smiles. Her missing tooth winks up at Blue.

There's a story in Starling City about Crook and Cassie. Blue heard the rumour himself more than once, from people who said they knew it as truth firsthand. The story says they killed a neighbour's cat, an animal sacrifice on Devil's Night. There's another story that says they have sex on fresh graves, and another that claims the reason Cassie is missing a tooth is that she broke it trying to bite into Crook's neck. Like a vampire.

Blue isn't sure about Cassie, doesn't know her well enough. But, at a party at Kevin Dyer's, Blue did see Crook once lure a racoon right into his hands with a peanut butter sandwich. They all watched from the back windows as the animal let Crook pick it up. When Crook had it between its hands, he snapped its neck—just like that. "Like breaking a twig," he'd said after. It was a summer's night and everyone was high on speed, hearts moving too fast to feel any grief until after the fact.

Crook is still in the shower, the water still running. Cassie rolls over onto her back. Beneath her sweatshirt, you can see the shape of her big, soft breasts melting across her chest. She exhales a long plume of smoke towards the ceiling. A faint bass line pounds on the wall from Dustin's room next door. Cassie looks over at Blue again, then to Aldea. "Okay," she says. "Let's go outside. I'll get dressed."

She looks at Blue and points to her cup. "You sure you don't want some wine while you wait? You know how long Crook takes in the shower."

Blue stares for a beat. "Actually, I will have some," he says, hoping that the hair of the dog will work its magic. Cassie's big bottle is still half-full, a cheap brand of table wine that comes in nothing less than one-and-a-half litre servings. Blue drinks straight from the bottle.

"Easy," Cassie says, grabbing the wine back. "I said you could have a sip, not finish the whole thing."

"No, you just asked me if I wanted some."

Cassie rolls her eyes. "Fuck, whatever. I don't care." She fills her glass again and rubs at her eyes. She sniffles as she pulls on a pair of jeans and struggles to zip up their broken fly. Her bottom lip is quivering.

"Oh, come on, don't cry," Blue says. "It's not a big deal."

"I'm just so tired of being treated like shit by everyone," she says.

Aldea puts a hand on Cassie's arm. "The birds can take

that away for you. They know how to take someone's sadness and turn it into their songs. You won't feel a thing after. Let me show you."

After the girls leave, Crook walks in with a towel around his waist. Blue is pouring himself another glass of wine.

"Hi," Crook says. He unwraps his towel and dries himself off, making sure to spend extra time between his legs, making sure Blue sees everything. Crook throws the towel over the back of his desk chair. A cloud of ash from the ashtray puffs up, scatters throughout the room. "How much do I owe you?" Crook asks. He wipes a hand through his wet hair, which hangs long past his shoulders.

"Twenty," Blue says. He's sweating. The room is warm, tight. The smells are only getting stronger. He's starting to think the wine was a mistake.

"Right, twenty." Crook finds his wallet in a pair of jeans he picks up off the floor, hands two tens to Blue. "Thanks, man."

"Yeah, no problem."

There are birds in the yard. Their chirping overthrows the Led Zeppelin CD that is still playing. Wings hit the window.

"What the fuck," Crook says. He looks outside. Blue reluctantly stands, feels relieved when his head stays together.

In the yard, Aldea and Cassie both have their arms raised. Aldea's mouth is moving, making a call that can't be heard above the flapping wings and screaming beaks and the relentless guitar sounds in the background.

The birds are descending. At first they look beautiful, perching on Cassie's shoulders and hands. And Cassie is smiling in a way that makes Blue realize he has never her smile before.

"Look how happy she is," he says to Crook.

And then there is a streak of red on Cassie's cheek, knocking her smile out of place.

The birds pile on. The blood comes fast and quick as they swoop in, hundreds of wings battering Cassie, pushing her to the ground. Their beaks are relentless, picking at flesh, picking until there is hardly anything left.

They scatter just as fast as they come, leaving a gap in the sky. That's when Blue and Crook see that they have taken Cassie's eyes and the soft fat of her cheeks. They have taken her hair for their nests and left her scalp red and raw. They have cleaned her arms and legs down to the bones and her mouth is crooked now, lower lip hanging by a thread, dropping to her chin.

And Aldea looks up at the window then and waves at Blue. Waves as though everything is fine, waves the way someone would just to say hello.

Blue leaves the room, feeling Crook's undressed body pointing towards him. But he doesn't want Crook to follow him, so he closes the door fast and hard behind him. Blue runs to the washroom on the way to the staircase. The mirror still wears steam from Crook's shower. Blue locks the door, runs the tap water, and throws up into the toilet.

He sits on the edge of the bathtub afterwards, catching his breath, taking tiny sips of water from the tap. He looks at himself in the mirror and washes his face. What have I done? He starts to wonder, but doesn't allow himself the time to answer. He knows the stories of other people's magic, knows that sometimes sacrifices are made, and fear must be put to the side. Blue knows there are prices to pay to become a vampire. *Think of what this will mean one hundred years from now*, he tells himself. *Nothing. It will mean nothing, because this memory will be a blip in the length of my life. The tiniest moment.*

Blue takes another deep breath before leaving the bathroom, trying not to think any harder than this unless he scratches too far under his own surface and finds himself unpersuaded by his own inner dialogue.

Downstairs, he expects chaos, ambulances and panic. But Troy and Sandy are still watching their movie, the volume up so high they didn't hear a thing. And Cassie didn't scream, did she? No, she smiled, and never ran, never fought the birds off.

As though she wanted it to happen. Invited it, even.

That's what Blue tries to convince himself of when he gets to the backdoor. Aldea is already waiting for him there. Crook has not come down yet. Maybe he is on the phone with the police.

"Come," Blue says, taking Aldea by her arm, pulling her down the driveway. His fingers touch the bone of her elbow, his thumb in the velvety crook of her arm. The places where last night's crimes began. He feels his body turning against him again, sickness rising. He makes it to the next block before throwing up into a garbage can.

16
Thin Metal Jesus

On the way back to Blue's apartment, Aldea keeps talking about Cassie and the birds. She wants Blue to know that she did it for Matter: "He was asking for it. He needed it. For growth."

And then: "This is how it will be for you, too, you know. If He comes, which He will. He's already here, listening. Ready for you. He just needed the strength. You will too, one day. You will know what it's like to be hungry like Him."

Matter, matter, what does it matter? Normally, Blue would be excited to hear something like this. But he doesn't feel hungry right now. Instead, his stomach is sour and cramped. It doesn't help that he has a wicked headache, and the sunlight overhead feels like it's drilling through the top of his skull. When he finally gets home, Blue tells Aldea to get under his bed and stay there for a while.

The sun disappears behind the clouds moments after they get inside. It's as though nature is taunting him today. It will rain in a couple of hours. Blue goes to the kitchen. A few roaches scatter when they see him. Normally he would try to chase them down but he doesn't have it in him right now. He takes a pitcher from the cupboard and fills it with ice and water. He holds it to his face first, which burns with sunlight and unease. He takes a glass to drink from and walks back to his room. He's relieved to see Aldea has hidden herself.

Blue punches the play button on his CD player. Robert Smith's mournful voice streams out of the speakers, the sound of love tangled in a spider's web. Blue lays back on his bed, tussles his hair with his fingers. It lands flat and thick around his head, hanging heavy. Girls always tell him how much they love his hair. He always wishes it could be bigger, weirder. Like Robert Smith's, teased and ratted.

Blue opens the drawer of his nightstand. In it he keeps a razorblade, a black candle, and a rosary he stole off a headstone in the cemetery last year. Blue still feels guilty about that, but he did it because he read about a character in a book who had done the same thing. Every time he looks at it, though, he wonders if there is a spirit attached to those beads who wants them back.

Blue sits up, puts the rosary around his neck and lights the black candle. He stares at the flame, takes the rosary's thin metal Jesus and sticks it in his mouth. A metallic taste blooms across Blue's tongue. He holds the razor blade to his skin inside his arm and bites down on the cross, bracing for the deceptive sting—thin red line with the kiss of a snake. Blood blossoms from the cut, which is deep enough to seep full, round drops.

Blue had to learn how to cut with the right amount of pressure. There are scars from the times he went a little too deep. Like that night at Kevin Dyer's when Blue was drunk on Wild Turkey and the blade sliced through him like butter.

All the tea towels in the kitchen got ruined: They ended up as bandages for Blue's arm. But the cut had become a flood, the blood relentless in its flow. Blue had to be driven to the hospital for stitches and fainted when they pulled into the parking lot.

That wound had left the biggest scar, but there were many others trailing up and down his arms. Some cuts had been too shallow to do much of anything—no evidence, and little blood. Some of the cuts were deep enough to hurt because that was what Blue had wanted at the time.

Now, he runs his finger along the opening in his skin and rubs his blood against the candle. He stares into the flame again and whispers some old words he memorized from an old book. Words that he speaks desperately, knowing that Samantha is listening nearby. Blue tries not to think about his sister right now, though. He has to hold his focus for this prayer to work. Because there is no turning back at this point. Blue needs Matter to do more than hear him: He needs Matter here, now.

The words creak and groan in his mouth like rusted door hinges and crooked floors. They crackle with time and dust and the trepidation of superstition that gets buried deep within the bones. They sound like curses and call to the one that Blue believes can change all the answers. These words leave his throat sore and his mouth dry and even though he doesn't know exactly what they mean, he knows how they feel, which is like fire and power and the promise of something new.

Blue prays until he's spitting words, until there's foam at

the corners of his mouth. He prays long after the CD in the stereo has stopped playing and long after the rain has hit his windows.

All over the city, people like Julie and Blue are getting ready for tonight. They are the ones calling each other on the phone, repeating the names of the clubs on King Street:

The Vixen!
The Spider!
The Lair!

They are cramming in close to dirty mirrors, applying another coat of red lip shade or painting their mouths glossy black. Collectively sipping on various cocktails to get a buzz before getting to the bar. Dresses and t-shirts come on and off again, as minds change about which look is going to be just right for tonight.

Everyone is piling on jewelry like armour. Silver rings are slipped onto fingers. Baubles and bangles are plucked from jewellery boxes. Symbols of bats and swords and stars dangle off earlobes. On go the layers of crosses and rosaries, salvaged from thrift stores or stolen from gravestones. No one worries too much about the wrinkles and rips and tears in their second-hand clothing, or the runs in their stockings. It will all disappear under the dim lights and thick smoke of the Vixen! The Spider! The Lair! Places where everything can become glamourous. Even the cheapest drugstore lipstick and the shakiest smudges of eye shadow become spells of beauty.

The darkness is generous with what it hides.

And then there's the communal spell that's ever being woven together here: The allure of becoming something *other*, of being changed by an unearthly creature. Of dying from a vampire's kiss and waking up tomorrow as something new, eternal.

The denizens of Starling City's secret clubs and hidden bars pull on their leather jackets and velvet blazers as they check their reflections in the mirror one last time before heading out the door. They meet each other at cafes first, and collect in booths at the Dominion Diner. They gather on street corners and run into one another on the buses they take to King Street. They walk in the middle of the roads as though they own the city because tonight, they do.

The Vixen! The Spider! The Lair! They keep these names close to their lips the same way they do their worn spells and charms. They scrawl lipstick messages across the night's sky asking: Who will I meet? What will happen?

Tomorrow, many will wake up with hangovers and heartbreaks. Others will find their shins and hips bruised from where they bumped drunkenly against chairs and tables as the night wore on. But it's always worth it, these minor sacrifices for the chance to be part of a myth. Or to become the legend itself.

Julie calls Blue. The phone rings and rings. She's about to hang up when he finally answers.

"You ready?" she asks. They had planned to meet

downstairs, outside her apartment.

"I'll be there soon," Blue says. He sounds sad, or tired. Julie asks if he's okay, but he hangs up. She tries not to be hurt by this: He didn't know I was still talking, she tells herself.

The rain has gotten heavier. The streets are sheets of water. Julie checks the time and opens a bottle of wine. She turns on the stereo, applies another coat of lipstick, debates on whether she should change her outfit. Tonight she's wearing a leather skirt that's a little too tight in the waist, but she bought it anyway because it was on sale.

The weather lets up by the time Blue calls her from the payphone at the corner. Julie looks out her window and sees Aldea outside, too, looking up at her. Julie waves but Aldea doesn't wave back.

Outside, Blue pulls out two cigarettes and lights them both, hands one to Julie.

"What did you do today?" she asks. Blue stares at the ground. Aldea doesn't seem to be listening.

"I'd rather hear about your day," Blue says, taking Julie's hand. His palm is sweating, or maybe it's just wet from the rain. He thinks of what it will feel like to hold hands once they're both vampires: What will it feel like to touch each other's bodies? Not like this, Blue imagines, for he's sure that vampires don't sweat. No, he assumes a vampire's skin stays cool and dry and smooth to the touch. Always perfectly composed.

"Your eyeliner is running," Julie says to him.

"It's okay," Blue says. "I like it a little smudged."

When they turn onto King Street someone in a group ahead whoops and yells and claps their hands. A beer bottle gets passed around before breaking on the sidewalk. Further down the street girls with short skirts and painted faces walk alone, and walk fast, with their heads down and their purses held tight. These girls slink in and out of the shadows, moving on sharp heels that give them away with the faintest of click-click-click-clacks. People gather in doorways to smoke joints and share flasks and even though there are unspoken expectations that everyone who comes to the clubs on King Street will be quiet and careful and cautious not to draw too much attention, it's hard not to on some nights.

Especially this night, when the air is charged with an electric buzz that runs through every breath you take. It's the feeling of possibility that comes with the spring season. The feeling of excitement when you know—you just *know*—that something is going to happen tonight.

Julie feels it in her stomach, which is doing so many flips that she's wondering if she should have had that wine before she left her house tonight.

Blue feels it in his hands, too, which are sweating so much now he lets go of Julie's grasp even though he wants to hold on to her. When they get to the Lair, Aldea goes straight inside. Julie holds back with Blue. "Are you okay?" she asks.

"I just wasn't feeling very well earlier," Blue says. "I'm better now, though." He wants to tell her about what happened to Cassie. And what it feels like to have raised the dead and then sleep with a walking corpse beneath your bed. And what it feels like to kiss one.

But Julie looks so worried, and then so relieved, by the simple statement he has already given that Blue can't bring himself to say more. So he doesn't.

If you hang out at the Lair, you can tell time by what is happening in the room. The regulars always know it's past midnight when the toilets overflow. By one A.M., the water is running out into the hallways where the payphone is.

Tonight doesn't feel as late as it is, but time must be slipping. Julie's bladder is full and there's a small line-up of girls ahead of her and everyone's tiptoeing around the questionable wetness on the tile floor. Girls in black velvet bellbottoms are hiking up their pants so they don't drag through the mess. Others clutch their long black skirts. People smoke as they wait and the air in the toilets is thick and unmoving.

People have drawn inverted crosses on the bathroom walls, and demons with red lipstick. And there are words, too—so many words. Some are illegible, words on top of words, or words misspelled or scrawled backwards so as to be a mystery. Julie always likes to read the walls, finding new oracles every time she comes.

Language doesn't always have to be a straight line, does it? What would it do to your mind to have your words flow from you in circles or squares instead of narrow passages parallel to the floor beneath you? What would bend within us, and around us, if our words were built differently?

What kind of magic would come closer to the surface? There is magic here, Julie has no doubt. She focuses on a short phrase and dares herself to memorize it:

"Make a wish when a train passes overhead and the nearest god will grant it."

Back out in the club, a band is setting up on stage. Blue is standing off to the side, waiting for Julie. He has bought her a fresh glass of wine, full to the brim. She takes a sip. A little spills out over the side of mouth, a red tear that Blue leans over and laps up. Julie smiles at this.

On stage, the first chord is struck. The drums kick in. People clap, then sway to the music. Their layers of silver chains and dangling earrings clack and flash to the beat. The lights turn from red to blue to purple to white, swirling the room together. Julie's head swims a little from the wine, which she is drinking too fast now. She wants to empty it so she can put down the glass and free her hands, move them through the air, thread them around Blue.

"Where is Aldea?" Julie asks.

"I think I saw her near the back, talking to someone," Blue says.

Julie asks another question, but Blue can't hear her over the music rumbling off the stage. It's for the best: Blue knows what Aldea is doing. She told him all about it on their way over to Julie's.

The club rumbles. Feet stomp. The singer sings. The room heats up. The sweat of so many bodies collects on the low ceiling. Fat drops of condensation drip back onto the bodies below. The lights change the colour of the singer's hair, which is bleached blonde. Opposite to so many in the audience who pour inky black dyes over their heads. The singer's voice rises and falls over jagged guitars and slinking keyboards. "I'm just a breath away from death today…" he cries, and people's hands rise and their mouths mimic the words back:

> *I'm just a breath away from death today.*
> *I'm just a breath away from death today.*
> *I'm just a breath away from death today.*

People sway and rock, fidgeting with their dangling silver charms and chugging their beers. There are times when ritual happens naturally, when a moment becomes sacred and every hook and wire connects into place. Like the graffiti in the bathroom, the language of body heat and collective song becomes a circle that allows for deeper magic.

It feels like no time at all before the band is starting their last song. Blue and Julie have both drunk at least a bottle of wine each by now.

The band always saves this song for the end because it is the song that everyone comes to hear.

It's familiar because it uses so many of the words and phrases found on the bathroom stalls of places like this. It's a song that doesn't come to you, but through you, because it speaks to so much of what everyone is already waiting for.

The song is called "Matter."

17
Call and Response

Aldea can hear His name on the lips of those who speak it here in the Lair. It sits there like a wet, fat fruit waiting to be eaten. So many of His believers in one place. Surely, He will come tonight.

Aldea can already feel it.

The spirits of Starling City can, too. They can know everything, if they want to. Many of them listen because what else is there to do when you are dead? Some of them taunt Aldea, and others encourage her. There are the ghosts of those who once believed in Him and have not yet lost their allegiance. There are others who tell Aldea to turn around and go back to the woods, go back to being a little lost girl who couldn't fend for herself the first time around.

All Aldea has to do is stand at the centre of the dance floor and read lips to watch them speak His name. She hears it carried in the music that sweeps the room, and in answer, calls them all to her. Her hair matches the bleached head of the young man moaning into the microphone. Normally people would stare at hair so white, but too many are mesmerized by the one on stage, lost in song and drifting on red wine highs.

Belief makes anything stronger. Any god, any ghost. It's all they need. It's why some gods reign longer than others. Their power comes from those who make them offerings, build temples and shrines.

Matter doesn't have His own official temple, but places like this do just as well. The band may as well be singing hymnals, their fans a congregation, shouting back in prayer. Call and response.

It doesn't take long for Aldea to catch the eye of the one she wants: She sees him at the edge of the dance floor. Long dark hair, big eyes. He smiles at her first. She moves closer to him.

They move together to the back of the room. Aldea offers to buy him a drink. She has money and pills, all stolen from Blue when he was in the shower earlier today. She slips two pills into a bottle of beer.

The man is beautiful, as Matter should be. He tells her his name is David, but Aldea doesn't need to know this. He won't be needing his name for much longer, will answer to a different one soon. Aldea lets him kiss her. She likes it, just as she liked the way Blue's kiss felt the night before. She knows that in David's eyes, she's just another girl at the club looking for a boyfriend. Aldea asks him to kiss her again. His lips bring back familiar memories of men she knew long before, in her previous life. *Soon, soon* says a voice in the back of her mind. Soon she will be the young woman she once was: As warm and alive as anyone else in this room right now.

The pills are working their magic. David is asleep before

the band's set is done. In the back of the club, it's easy to kill someone without being noticed. Everyone's eyes are on the stage, or on each other. The backs of the booths here are high, made for privacy, made for spaces where you can get away with things no one needs to know about. It's nothing for Aldea to hold David's head in her hands and twist his neck fast and hard, feeling the vibration of its breaking bones.

Aldea kneels on the floor, knocks three times. Says a prayer to the black dog Hekate to raise the dead: "Mother mediator, before whom the gods tremble, bitch of the blackest nights, barking at woven roads, I tell you that we want it badly enough, mother. Make Him rise! Make Him real! Make Him rise! Make Him real!" Aldea shouts this last bit, confident the razor-sharp guitar solo coming out of the speakers covers her voice.

Aldea feels for the man's pulse. Nothing.

Aldea knocks again on the floor: One, two, three.

She takes candles from nearby tables and sets them all in a circle in front of David. She pulls a strand of hair from her head and shoves it into his mouth and says, "Taste this. Remember me. You promised to come back. You told me to remember you. Who will remember you if you do not come to us?"

Aldea puts her fingers back on David, feeling for a pulse again. There's a flutter beneath the skin now, faint but growing. And then a flutter behind the eyes, too.

David vomits a little. Normal for a corpse. It's such a shock to wake again, especially full of liquids your body no longer needs, or knows what to do with. But it's a good sign. David's broken neck is already repairing itself as it prepares for a second life.

Aldea helps him to the bathroom, which is miraculously empty with everyone enamoured by the music. The possession is upon him. But first, the purge.

Anyone walking in will just think Aldea's helping a boyfriend who had too much to drink.

"Easy, easy," she says, rubbing his back.

A ghost knocks against the bathroom stall. "I can do that too. I can take over anyone I want at any time."

"You're jealous," Aldea says. "You know this is not just another ghost in here." The spectre frowns, fades into the wall.

"Let's clean you up," Aldea says to the one who is becoming Matter. "You must be hungry."

"I am," He says, and when Aldea looks into His eyes, she knows He's there. The one everyone's been waiting for, the one who can even save someone like Aldea.

18
Kiss of the Moon

The room feels likes it has expanded, stretched by the live music that ended moments ago. Everyone is giddy on red wine and adrenaline.

Blue and Julie find Aldea in the biggest booth in the club. She is not alone. The man she is with is beautiful. Aldea has a smile at play on her lips, and a look in her eye. She slides out of the booth and clamps her hands onto Blue and Julie's shoulders, brings her face right up into theirs: "This is it," she says. "He's here." A thread gets pulled through the eye of the needle again.

The body that used to belong to someone named David motions for Blue and Julie to sit. Julie slides in first. She likes how it feels to take up so much space. It seems the entire room is watching them now, wondering: Who are those people with that beautiful man? What is it about him that attracts the gaze?

But it can't be real. Blue and Julie both have met people before who said they are vampires. Dime a dozen around here. Especially in a place like this, where people dress up just to look the part.

Julie sits next to Matter and is drugged on His words and the kiss of magic as he slips an arm around her shoulders. His voice is smooth and deep, as dark as the red wine they serve at the bar. Electric veins beneath His skin, the ticking of a watch on His wrist tickling her ear. Around them the old building groans and pops and stretches to accommodate the surge of dancers on the floor. The band is packing up on stage and the DJ is cranking the music full blast. Outside, birds stir from their midnight slumber in the eaves troughs. They twitter and flutter together in hurried circles, laughing like children sneaking out of their beds in the middle of the night.

The birds fly through the door as people come and go. They sit and watch from the exposed pipes that run along the ceiling. They have come to see Matter, who they have heard so much about. Some of their friends met His mistress earlier today. Their claws sound like bare feet whispering on wooden floors but no one can hear this, the way they cling to their perches. The birds look at Matter's hair, which hangs to the middle of His back. What beautiful nests they could build!

And now they titter as Matter puts His face against the girl's neck.

Julie lets Him. This is the only way to know whether it's real (and she so badly wants this to be real). The candles flicker and sputter on the table. Wax spills. This close, Matter feels like a fever, cold and hot all at once. He starts first by kissing her. His lips are so slow and soft she doesn't feel the first cut His teeth make. He doesn't bite or clamp like she expects him to. Instead, it starts as a razor-thin opening, His feeding place is as gentle as the kiss.

He tastes from her, drinks what He can. The first drink in a new body is always the best. It's also the most dangerous. It's easy to forget the subtleties of life, the fragility of a heart. But with the taste of fire and copper running through His mouth, Matter remembers how to take what He needs. For this body, which is now His body, is still bound by its own rules: He cannot drink endlessly just yet, must allow for time to adjust. But soon, soon. For now, he must satiate His hunger slowly.

When Matter returns to earth like this, He is bound by limitations like all other living things.

And the oaths that run through people's veins: Matter hears the patter of prayers as His spirit wanders the streets, but it's different to hear the way they echo through the blood. The way they pound through His head as Julie's blood rushes into His mouth, as hungry for Him as He is for her.

The ones who love Him always want to be like Him, but they can't. They aren't close enough to being gods, and the magic that made Matter this way has been lost and gone for so long there's no finding it again. But He can give them a taste of what it's like: Just a tiny touch, a temporary life between their world and His, which helps Him to thrive here. Because once Matter has taken from you, the two of you are tied. You feed, and you feed Him. Whatever you give yourself, He takes.

"Listen, listen," the shadows remind Him now, and

Matter listens for the heartbeat that pushes itself into His throat. Something else comes to back to His memory: The way young girls wear death on their faces. He knows the taste and smell of it long before it hits, even in the dark of a club like this. The girl in His arms reminds Him of a love He had long ago. One of the few memories that stays with Him; a ghost that clings close, a remembrance that He allows, maintains space for.

Matter pulls away, still cupping Julie's head under one hand. Blue watches as Matter brushes the hair from Julie's face, so gently: Blue is jealous in more ways than one.

And Julie? What is happening to her as the club writhes and swirls and she fades away in a booth in the back? She has left the Lair and gone back to the woods, back to the house where they found Aldea. There, she rests on the bare floorboards in a small room. Up above, the birds sing and chirp against the ceiling, circling her, wings flapping against her face to satisfy themselves that she is not waking up.

No: Julie is dreaming within a dream. She is dreaming that she is asleep in her old bed, the one she grew up in out in the suburbs, the one that was down the hall from her parents' bedroom. The one that was tucked beneath a slanted ceiling that always made her feel small and cozy and protected. In Julie's dream, she's sleeping there, deeper with every breath. She's sinking into the mattress. Her arms and legs are getting heavy—so heavy she couldn't lift them if she wanted to.

But she doesn't want to. The bed is doing her breathing for her now, pulling her deeper into the blankets, pulling her down until there's nothing but rest.

And then the scene changes: The birds are back. At first, they sound as though as they are outside, high, high in the trees. But then they are in Julie's ear, their beaks plucking at her hair, tugging at the corners of her t-shirt. Their wings get beneath her elbows and armpits and they pull Julie up, up, out of her body, sending her soaring out over the woods, which are dark and shimmering beneath her. She sees the river and a pale coyote walking the path. She looks up above and sees the stars, brighter and clearer than she's ever seen them before. Behind her, the moon presses its mouth against the roof of the house, its white lips kissing the windows and walls, trying to make its way inside.

In the movies, vampires always seem to drink so much from their victims. The drinking scenes go on for what feels like forever. But in reality, it's only seconds: the dream state a victim enters may feel much longer, though. Just like a dream you may have while asleep: What takes seconds for your subconscious to generate may unfold in what feels like hours. But people can only lose so much blood so fast.

Julie is out of Matter's arms much quicker than it seems, and Matter has room for more. He turns to Blue, whose body has gone stiff, awkward. After all this time imagining, manifesting, visualizing this moment, Blue can't bring himself to respond the way he thought he would. He wants to bend and ply, like Julie. He wants to feel seduced, like in the movies where people go limp, trusting in the strength of the embrace.

Still, the moment presses forward. Matter is reaching for

Blue all the same, oblivious or uncaring as to how Blue's body responds. It makes no difference whether someone fights or gives in, anyway: Matter is strong. Blue can feel this strength in the way His hands move up and down Blue's arms. "Relax," Matter says. Aldea bounces eagerly in the booth, impatient for this to get on. Blue imagines what it all looks like from across the room: Beautiful people having each other, dark dances in dangerous places.

"Relax," Matter says again, brushing Blue's hair away. Blue lets himself rest his forehead against Matter's shoulder, then dares to kiss His neck. Matter laughs a little at this and Blue is relieved. And then, in a blink, Matter's mouth is on Blue. Blue closes his eyes and sees a dream of black lace and blue eyes. He smells cloves and dark cherry incense as something comes to lift him off the ground: an angel with black hair and white wings, red leaking from its throat.

19
Old Hag Syndrome

They all take a cab back to Julie's. Julie undresses the moment they get through the door: She has never been so tired. She leaves a trail of black clothing from the front hall to her bedroom. Blue gets into bed fully dressed, boots on.

To Julie, everything is heightened: The smell of the sweat of the club on her skin, the cigarette smoke in her hair. The dampness of her underwear pressed high between her legs all night. Is it true that vampires don't have any odours? Is it true that if you become one, your body no longer holds onto its old functions—you never have to go the bathroom, or buy another stick of deodorant, or bathe unless you really want to? Julie lets these familiar questions roll through her head and wonders what she will be like when she wakes in the morning.

Down the hall, Aldea and Matter talk. Their voices are low but make their way through the walls all the same. The conversation is brief. The apartment door opens and closes. Julie only hears one set of footsteps going downstairs. Her eyes are heavy but she won't let them shut yet: She gets up and looks down the hall. Aldea is in the bathroom, washing her hands and face. "He left," Aldea says.

"But He'll be back, right?" Julie asks.

Aldea looks at the floor. "I hope so," she says.

Julie wants to register this but her mind is ready to dream. All she can do is nod. "Okay," she says.

"Can I stay here tonight?" Aldea asks. "I don't feel like going all the way back to the woods right now."

"Sure," Julie says. She's already turning away from Aldea and is closing the door before the dead girl folds herself up and slides underneath the couch.

Back in bed, the sheets feel cool against Julie's legs, which are burning as though they've been in the sun for hours. She stretches out and feels a dull ache across her lower back. It stretches down into her knees and pulses through her calves. Despite the heat coming off her body, Julie shivers. She wants to roll over and reach for Blue, but doesn't have the strength. Instead, she lays still, her mind drifting away on a silver river.

Dreams come in through the drafts in the windows.

Something appears at the foot of Julie's bed. It stands tall and dark with an aura of pewter around it: The shape of a cloaked body. It carries the smell of mildew and frankincense, a perfume that tickles the nose and knots the stomach. Outside the window the streets are still dark. Julie and Blue are dreaming the same dream and both are too weak to move when the ghost bends down and drinks from each of them. There is a throb of pain, the pressure under cold, impossible lips.

Their hearts race. They stare at the ceiling, exhausted and

frozen in place. Just a fever dream, they tell themselves, as the light from a car going by flashes across the ceiling.

Back in full force and free to roam, Matter walks the city streets late into the hours. His new body is adapting, stretching, becoming something Other.

The night birds sing: He has returned! The moon smiles. And the rooms and walls that hold His prayers whisper His name, calling Him from all corners, helping Him find His way.

He follows the paths of lonely people sitting in late night bars. He invites them to talk, to walk, and when they follow, He takes away their pain and leaves their bodies to rest in laneways.

In the nights to come, people will swear they feel something crawling across the foot of their beds. Brushing lightly against their skin. Candles that were blown out come alight again. There's a smell of myrrh and pine, dark soil and copper that seems to linger throughout the city, a perfume that somehow cuts through the smog and smoke of Starling City.

20
Wet Stains

Blue and Julie take their time waking up. It's late afternoon by the time they get out of bed. Julie can't remember if she is supposed to be at work today.

Does it matter anymore? She hasn't decided yet.

She thinks again: No, her next shift is tomorrow.

It's a good thing, too. The light creeping in from behind the curtains is the colour of four o'clock. They have slept all day.

Julie feels into her toes and hands. Blue hugs himself, running his hands over his arms. The way you might feel yourself out the day after losing your virginity, or celebrating a birthday, wondering: Am I supposed to feel different?

They both decide that they feel the same. Julie looks at herself in the mirror. It's hard to tell if she's changed. The curtains are drawn too tight, the light seeping through, too faint. She is afraid to open them, but Blue dares to, just to see what will happen.

Soft light flows in. No one goes up in flames.

Julie looks tired and her hair is greasy. She forgot to wash her face before going to bed. Last night's eyeliner sticks to the corners of her eyes.

Blue takes his boots off, sighs at the relief of having them off his feet after sleeping in them. He smells his own sweat and pulls the boots back on fast, before Julie notices. She's too busy looking at her teeth in the mirror: "I think they look a little longer. They definitely feel sharper. Definitely," she says, running her finger over her eye teeth.

Blue waits in bed while Julie showers. When she comes back out, he unwraps the towel from her body and pulls her into the sheets. Her hair leaves dark, wet stains on the pillowcases as Blue pins her beneath him.

They kiss and grab at each other, then playfully bite and clamp harder. "Is it working?" Blue asks as Julie's teeth takes hold of him. He doesn't want to let on how much it hurts.

"I don't think so," Julie says. "The skin won't break."

"Maybe Matter can show us what to do," Blue says.

"But how? Where did He go?"

"He's already answered us once. We'll call Him back again," Blue says, though he's guessing at what's supposed to happen next. Not wanting to linger too long on the uncomfortable questions forming in the back of his mind, Blue nips again at Julie's skin, then pulls her underwear down to her ankles. She raises her hips for him, and Blue buries his face in her warmth.

They finish with flush faces and sweat running down their backs. They dress in loose t-shirts and jeans, and then go out to the living room to wake Aldea. Julie kneels on the carpet by the couch and calls Aldea's name softly.

There's no answer. Blue puts four slices of bread in the toaster and turns on the coffee maker. He flips the stations on the radio until he finds a good song.

"Aldea?" Julie calls again, a little louder this time. Reluctantly, she reaches under the couch. She can't imagine how Aldea fit herself under there to begin with. If it wasn't for the fact that Aldea's long, white hair was streaming out from under the sofa now, Julie would have thought that she had imagined seeing the girl press herself beneath it.

Julie touches something wrong. Her hand recoils, and then she peeks under the couch again. "Aldea?" she asks, more quietly this time. Carefully, Julie reaches out again. Her hand wraps around something hard and smooth: A bone.

The bone is long, part of a limb. Julie holds it gingerly across her lap. When Blue sees it he drops the mugs he is taking out of the cupboard. They break across the floor. "Holy shit," he says, rushing to Julie's side. Blue picks up one end of the couch, tilting it to give Julie a better look.

"Oh my god," Julie says. Aldea's bones are all here, her long white hair spilled around her. Something dark, the residue of what was Aldea's flesh, stains the clothes they had stolen for her. Julie collects the bones into a neat pile on the coffee table.

"I can't believe it," she says. "He didn't change her."

"Maybe He couldn't," Blue says.

They wrap Aldea's bones in the ceremonial cloth that Julie showed Blue the first time he came here. "Let's eat before we leave," Blue says. "I'm starving." And he means it. There's an all-consuming hunger in the pit of his stomach.

He pours ketchup onto his plate to dip his toast into. Julie slathers her's with butter and jam. They both take big bites, trying to ignore the dead girl's bones just six feet away.

Blue spits his food back onto his plate. Everything in his mouth has turned to ash. Julie is more patient. She finds a napkin before clearing the contents from her mouth.

Their tongues taste of fire and myrrh. Blue tries another bite, as though the first was a mistake. The same thing happens: Everything turns to dust.

"Shit," Julie says. "You know what this means."

"Something happened," Blue says. "We changed."

"But into what?"

There is nothing in Julie's fridge that will help them. No uncooked meats or bones to suck on.

"Here," Julie says, hurrying to find the sharpest knife in her drawer. "Try this." And she cuts her wrist, fast and hard and excited. "Drink," she says, pressing the cut to Blue's mouth.

Blue holds Julie's arms with both hands and as his tongue prods the cut. It's shallow, but enough to feel the coppery heat of what's beneath Julie's skin. His throat accepts it.

"Holy shit," Blue says again.

"Let me try," Julie says, and Blue opens himself to her.

They grab each other's hands and jump up and down the living room. Someone from the apartment below bangs on the walls. They ignore it and keep bouncing like little kids.

The rules don't apply anymore.

This is it. Julie and Blue are both something else now, something Other.

21
The Rules They Have Followed So Far

1. Snap your fingers three times before bed and say His name nine times before you state the following: "I will meet you in my dreams and give you anything you want." (Whatever He asks for must be given within the next fifty years of your life.)

2. Stand in front of a mirror. Apply a thick coat of black lipstick to your mouth. Stare at the centre of your forehead, into your third eye. Let your gaze soften. Lose your focus. Let your peripheral vision sink into the darkness of your lips. Relax your face. Let your mouth become a vehicle for the damned. Invite them to move your tongue, to pull words from your throat, to change the expression on your face. Let the spirits know you are willing to speak on their behalf and *so it is*!

3. Light a candle and leave it in your windowsill. If you are feeling brave prick your finger and anoint the candlestick with blood so that something may find you by your scent. Spirits get hungry, you know, especially when people forget what sustains them: Belief.

4. Believe. That's always the easiest spell. If you want Matter to appear, tell Him so. Capitalize the spelling of His name and any reference you give Him so that he feels treated like a god. Because He is, isn't He?

Isn't He?

The sunlight fights through the thickness of the trees that crowd in around Blue and Julie as they carry Aldea's bones through the woods. Small patches of sun dapple their hands and faces. Blue is grateful that he does not have to give up the light of day, grateful that it has turned out to be just a myth, even though Julie complains about the light hurting her eyes.

As they walk, they talk about the dreams that led them here: The promise of what they think it will mean to be young and beautiful always. The power of immortality. The freedom of staying up all night and never having to go to work in the morning. These spoken dreams weave through the roots and brush, finding their way down to the places where bodies rest in unmarked graves.

The birds stop singing when they get to the house. Inside, the light doesn't reach very far through the windows. Black rooms, thick as velvet and holding onto pieces of the night. Blue picks up a candle from the mantle and carries it downstairs as he and Julie descend into the basement.

The grave that Aldea dug herself out of is still open,

untouched. Julie carefully lays the bones down into it.

"Do we need to put her back together somehow?" she asks. Blue stares into the ground and shrugs.

"I wouldn't know how," he says.

Later, this will become a story in Starling City, too. Some of the rumours will say that Aldea was not dead at all: that she was buried alive after Blue and Julie became jealous of her relationship with Matter. That story will say that guilt ate away at Julie, drove her to confess to someone that she thought she had seen a twitch of life in Aldea's eyes and fingers as they covered her with dirt.

But these stories always become exaggerated with time. No one was in the room that night to see what went on except for Blue and Julie. Starling City is bloated with elaborations, mis-remembrances. Another story says Matter clung to the ceiling, a saturation of shadow watching as Blue and Julie put the girl back in her grave. Or that Matter rode in through the woods like fog because He wanted to be sure Aldea was truly gone.

Regardless of what Aldea had believed of Matter, He was never going to change her because there was nothing to her. A vampire can't feed off of someone who is already dead. She can't even bleed. If you had cut into her, the flesh would be as dry and white as her hair.

Julie tries to arrange Aldea as best she can, gently laying out her long leg bones, fixing her hair so that it hangs long and smooth around her. "I wish we had something to leave, flowers or wine or something," Julie says. Blue reaches into his pocket and pulls out a few silver coins, drops them into the grave. "For spiritual debts," he says, pushing the earth back over top of Aldea's remains.

At around the same time Julie and Blue are leaving the woods, some people in homes nearby start having visions and auditory hallucinations. They hear chants that sound like ancient tongues and when they close their eyes, they see a man with long, dark hair pulling the fabric of the night around himself like a cloak before plucking two stars from the sky to use as eyes.

22
Sacrifice

Julie gets ready for her shift at the pub. She takes her time getting dressed, putting on extra eyeliner and hanging mismatched earrings from her lobes. In the left ear, a long chain with a dangling bat at the end. In the right, a cubic zirconia stud—just one, something she found at a garage sale last summer.

Julie foregoes the turtleneck she usually wears and pulls on a tight black t-shirt instead. The collar dips in a "v" shape below her throat. She pulls sheer gray stockings over her legs and steps into a black denim skirt. She imagines what it will be like to walk into the restaurant, picturing heads turning as she enters, and her coworkers saying, "Something seems different about you."

She also thinks about the difficult customers who come in sometimes, and whether they will speak to her differently now. If there will be something about her that intimidates or enchants. Or whether it will even make a difference at all. *It's not like I'll have to work there much longer*, Julie reminds herself.

She wears sunglasses as she walks to the pub even though it's overcast. She wants to keep them on for her shift, but it's too dark in the restaurant to see. Julie is disappointed with herself. Night vision aborted.

The smell of food gets to her almost immediately. Salivating, Julie eyes plates of fries and eggs that are coming out of the kitchen. She dares to sneak a fingertip into a scoop of mashed potatoes and ends up swallowing ash, eyes watering as she tries not to choke on her way to table nine.

Her body starving, Julie panics for the first time: Am I really never going to eat anything again? She's not sure what she expected to feel, but didn't think it would be like this: a stomach full of cravings unable to be satisfied. She tells herself her body is still changing, still letting Matter's magic take hold.

The pub slows after lunch, the work crowds heading back to the office. Marion, one of the servers, sits at the bar and lights a cigarette. "You look good," she says. "Like you lost weight or something."

"Yeah?" Julie asks. She runs her tongue over her teeth to feel if they've become any sharper. "I feel a bit different than I used to."

"How so?" Marion asks, tipping her head back at the ceiling to let loose a long plume of smoke. Julie stares at her co-worker's neck: Is she supposed to be attracted to it? In the movies she always sees vampires staring at a pulse or a vein there, as though they can see beneath the skin or smell the blood below.

All Julie can smell is Marion's cigarette and the grease and beer that linger in the air. Still, she takes a careful step closer to Marion.

"Oh, you like my earrings?" Marion asks, misreading

Julie's body language. "I just got them at the flea market last weekend. It was so nice to finally have a Saturday off. You're working the same shifts as me this week, right?"

"Right," Julie says. "I think so. I should check the schedule again. And yeah, those earrings are cool—really cool."

Brian, their manager, walks in off his lunch break. He frowns at Marion's cigarette but she doesn't put it out. Even though customers smoke inside, the staff are supposed to smoke around the back. "It just doesn't look very professional," Brian always says.

This is around the time the afternoon drinkers trickle in. The tips are shit at this time of day because everyone's nursing pints and no one's ordering food. Marion gets busy rolling cutlery. Julie hides out in the back and waits for things to pick up.

Mac is the cook in the kitchen. He's worked here since the place opened twenty years ago. No one tells him what to do, not even Brian. When it's slow, Mac sits on a milk crate in the staff room and does crossword puzzles. That's where Julie finds him when she comes into the kitchen.

She opens the fridge quietly. There's a pile of raw steaks, fresh for the day and just delivered that morning. They have to be frozen, but Mac leaves that kind of work for the night crew. "All I do is cook the food, not take care of it," he likes to say.

Julie takes out a small steak. It's cold and slippery between her fingers and she holds it awkwardly, unsure of where to put her hands. She looks around again and bites down on it.

The meat is tougher than she expected. Her teeth do not go all the way through. In fact, they barely sink into the cold flesh at all.

But the juice, the blood. It runs down her chin and soaks into her shirt. It fills her mouth with salt and copper and she forces herself to swallow, relieved that it goes down rather than turning to soot.

She sucks again, working her mouth around the meat until it can't give her any more to drink. When she's done, she puts it in the trash, burying it deep into the garbage can so that it goes unnoticed. Surely Brian won't miss one little steak, but she's not sure: Does he count the inventory? Will anyone check?

But then Julie reminds herself again that she probably won't need this job for much longer, anyway. How many vampires have jobs? None that she can think of from the books she's read. And no reason to change that. She goes to the bathroom and looks in the mirror. Her face and skin look the same, her hair and nails, too. But soon, soon, it will all be different?

It has to be. Right?

Blue goes back to his apartment while Julie's at work. She invited him to stay at her place if he wanted to, but he needs a break and misses his own room and the CDs and candles and things he keeps as the sources of all of his small powers.

At home, he pulls out a shoebox from the top shelf of his closet and sits on the edge of his bed. The lid of the box is bent and falling apart at the seams, reliant on two elastic bands to help keep everything together. He unwinds the elastics, enjoying the musical notes they make as they slide off the cardboard. Inside, there are pictures of his sister. Samantha smiles out at him in a photo that neither he nor his mother took. It's of Samantha on a gravel driveway, laughing at the camera. A row of thick pines is behind her, the sky overcast. Her teeth are white against the dark purple lipstick she always wore. Sunglasses are pushed up on top of her head. Blue has looked at this photo a thousand times before, trying to imagine what his sister was laughing at in this moment. As though a joke was made and the flash went off, the image captured rather than performed.

Today he asks her out loud: "What was so funny?"

He waits for an answer. The wind blows in through the window behind him. A car honks outside. Blue looks around the room, feeling for his sister but finds nothing.

She is not coming today to answer him.

The phone rings. Blue jumps at the sound and is quickly embarrassed to be so scared. His face is going red as he answers, grateful no one can see him.

It's Kevin Dyer looking to score some pills. "I can be there in an hour," Blue says.

When the bus comes, Blue pays his fare with loose change and sits at the back. He looks out the window and reads the graffiti that goes by, trying to put it all together into a message. The city itself a grimoire, putting us all under its spell:

KILL. SLEEP LATER. NEVER WORK. I WAS HERE.

Blue lets each word roll around his tongue, silently holding them all inside. It only takes five stops for the bus to empty. No one is heading to the suburbs at this time of day. Blue enjoys being alone like this. He wonders if Kevin will be alone. He didn't mention that he had anyone over, but Kevin is rarely by himself. Usually when he wants pills is when he has company.

Blue is right: Zoriah and Rose are at Kevin's. Both of the girls are laying on a pile of pillows on the living room floor. They are only wearing bras and panties, except Rose, who is draped in a long black veil that hangs down to her ass. "It's cool, huh?" Zoriah asks when she sees Blue taking it all in. "Rose made it." Zoriah takes the stiff netting between her thick fingers. She has long fake nails with tiny white gems embedded in the tips. They look expensive. Rose smiles up at Blue. They've met before but Rose is always kind of quiet around him. Rose rolls on her back and pulls the veil up around her, an instant cocoon. She giggles.

"Don't mind them," Kevin says. "They got into the tequila about an hour ago."

"You wanna watch some TV or something?" Kevin asks. He picks up the remote and turns the channel to MTV. A Type O Negative video comes on. Kevin turns up the volume. Zoriah and Rose start to make out. One of them bumps their elbows on the coffee table and they both break out laughing. Kevin turns up the volume even more.

"What've you been up to?" Kevin asks.

Blue wants to tell him about Aldea and Matter and the rituals he's been doing. The things he has awoken. The changes that are happening within him. Instead, he shrugs. "Nothing much. Did you hear about what happened to Cassie?"

"Yeah, I heard she got attacked by a bunch of birds. Freak accident or something. Crazy. I didn't know her that well but she always seemed okay to me."

"I was there," Blue says. "It was pretty fucked."

"Shit," Kevin says, draining the last of his bottle of beer. "You want a drink or something?"

"Yeah," Blue says. "Whatever you got."

Kevin heads to the kitchen. Blue pulls the pills from his pocket and puts them on the table while Kevin's in the kitchen. Kevin drops a pile of bills down in exchange when he comes back with the beers.

"Ooh, candy!" Zoriah says when she hears Kevin crack open the little baggie of yellow and blue pills. "Can we have some?" Her and Rose crawl across the carpet on their knees and put their hands out like kids.

"Just one for now," Kevin says. "Remember last time you mixed these with tequila?"

Zoriah groans and rolls her eyes. "Yeah, I puked for hours," she says, looking at Blue. "It was disgusting." And then she laughs as she pops a pill into her mouth and swallows it in one go. "But I'm not that drunk today. Just a little buzzed." Her and Rose crawl away again, back into the little world they are in together.

Another video comes on. "I hate this song," Kevin says, changing the channel. He lands on a courtroom show. "I like stuff like this," he says. "The people on here are pretty funny sometimes."

Blue sips his beer. Usually he would drink it fast to get the buzz, but he likes Kevin's house. It's quiet and clean and there's always a lot to eat and drink.

"You hungry?" Kevin asks, as though reading Blue's thoughts.

"Starving," Blue says.

Kevin goes to the kitchen again, comes back with plates of cold pizza. Blue takes a bite, and it dissolves like sand between his teeth. "Fuck," he says, drinking his beer faster now to chase it away.

"You okay?" Kevin says.

"Yeah, I just remembered I'm not supposed to eat any dairy anymore. It's been giving me stomach aches."

"Shitty," Kevin says, taking Blue's pizza right out of his hand. "More for me, then."

The TV show ends. Zoriah and Rose have gone quiet: They are asleep in each other's arms, drooling into the carpet.

"You wanna go to the bar or something?" Kevin asks. "I'm kinda bored and those two will be passed out for a while."

They walk eight blocks to the sports bar. It's not the kind of place Blue or Kevin would normally hang out, but in the suburbs there aren't many choices.

The bar is dark and the two men at the counter stare at Blue and Kevin when they enter. They take a booth and the bartender yells over to them to order at the bar because there's no one on table service until dinner hour. Kevin gets up and returns with a pitcher of beer.

Twenty minutes later and Kevin's drunk. Blue is feeling nothing more than a little giddy.

"What do you think of Zoriah?" Kevin asks.

Blue shrugs. "She's okay. She's pretty."

"She always wants to go out with me," Kevin says. "And I know she's hot—she is, right? But I just can't see her like that. I don't like her that way I guess."

"Who do you like?" Blue wonders.

Kevin looks at the TV screen. There's a baseball game on. Someone has just hit a home run.

"I dunno," Kevin says. "Maybe I only like myself." He laughs then and Blue does, too.

When they finish their beer, they head back outside. The sun is white hot and blinding after being in the bar's darkness.

"You wanna see something cool?" Kevin asks, his speech slightly slurred.

"Sure," Blue says. He can feel the beer sloshing in his empty belly as he walks. His stomach growls in protest. It's so loud he's sure Kevin would hear it if it weren't for the noise of traffic to cover it up.

They walk towards the 7-11 two blocks away. Kevin leads Blue around the back where there's an alleyway full of garbage bins and cigarette butts. "I smoked a joint back here yesterday with my cousin and we found this," Kevin says, pointing around a big black garbage bag where the body of a dead raccoon melts into the pavement. "I've seen a lot of roadkill but nothing that was as rotten as this."

The fur is falling off the flesh, the flesh off the bone. Blue's mouth waters at the sight of blood.

Blue gets closer, as close as he can to stand the smell, and puts his fingers in the raccoon's mouth. He tugs hard and pulls out a tooth—sharp and yellow.

"Dude, you are crazy!" Kevin says.

"Maybe," Blue says. He pulls the tooth across his arm to see how sharp it is. A long, thin line of blood beads up. Blue runs his finger over the cut and drinks of his own life. Teased by the taste, his body demands more.

He takes Kevin's hand. Kevin lets him. Blue runs the tooth fast and hard across Kevin's arm. His friend flinches. The beer is keeping the edges soft. The sun shines on both of them and Blue feels lightheaded again, unsure of himself. Something inside reminds him he can stop if he wants to. But Kevin's blood is coming quickly. Blue's stomach growls again, even louder than before; Kevin hears it this time.

Blue has cut deeper than he thought he could with that tooth. Kevin's scared now, but Blue can hardly hear what he's saying. He puts his mouth to the wound fast and drinks as much as he can.

Kevin's trying to pull away, but Blue holds him tighter. Kevin's stronger and breaks free. "Dude, I told you stop. This shit's fun sometimes, but we've never done it like this. This is gonna leave a scar. And aren't you worried about rabies or something?" Kevin wads the bottom of his t-shirt together to soak up some of the blood. Adrenaline overrides any buzz. The world is no longer softening, but coming back into sharp focus. Kevin's arm is dripping all over the pavement and onto his shoes. It's on Blue's shoes, too, and running down his chin.

"You don't understand, Kevin," Blue says. "I tried to tell you earlier, but I knew it wouldn't make any sense. It's hard to explain even now, but I want you to trust me. Will you trust me?"

Kevin sits down on a milk crate. "I feel dizzy," he says. His face is white, hands shaking.

Blue kneels down and reaches for Kevin's arm again. He brings it to his mouth slower this time. He doesn't need more blood: The hunger has already been satiated enough. But Blue wants to try again. To see how far he can push it. To see if drinking more will change him in any way.

Kevin kicks at him. "Stop! I thought you were cool. Take me home. Just take me home. I think I'm gonna puke or pass out or something."

"Fine," Blue says. "Sorry. I just thought… I dunno what I thought."

"This better not leave a scar," Kevin says. He tries to stand up but can't. "I need a minute."

"Put your head between your legs," Blue tells him. "I saw that on TV once."

Kevin takes the suggestion. "People are going to be so freaked when they hear you did this to me," he's saying from between his knees. "You're done around here. This is fucked."

Blue's heart drops. "Oh, come on, Kevin," he says. "I

didn't mean to go so deep. This isn't so bad. Why is this different from any other time?"

"Because this time you scared me," Kevin says. "That is the big fucking difference. And if I have some kind of disease or something you're going to pay. For real." His voice is shaking now.

"Don't tell anyone, okay? Promise?" Blue asks. In all the times he's played out these scenarios in his head it's always so elegant, so easy: Easy to act upon what's within his (new) nature, easy to survive whether or not victims are willing. But so many people he knows talk as though they are willing to be bitten, to bleed. Kevin never gave Blue reason to think he'd fight like this. If anything, Blue thought he'd be hailed as a legend right now.

Kevin should be in his arms, limp and submissive. Not scared and angry and threatening to turn against Blue altogether. Blue thinks of some of his favourite movie scenes and asks himself: What would a vampire do? A single thought responds: *Vampires kill!*

There's a rock by the back door of the 7-11, something the staff used to keep the door propped open when they're on break. Blue picks it up and takes a breath before bringing it down on the back of Kevin's head.

Kevin doesn't see it coming, so he doesn't scream or fight. Already faint, he falls to the ground. Blue was not expecting this—though he isn't sure what he thought would happen. He brings the rock down onto Kevin's head again, and again, and again. He does it fast, worried that someone could see him at any moment. But at this time of day, there's no one around. That's the thing about the suburbs: They're terrible places to be in danger, because no one is ever nearby to save you.

When Kevin has stopped breathing, Blue brings his tongue to his friend's bleeding head. He takes a careful taste first and then puts his entire mouth on the wound. He takes in hair and skin, forcing himself to suck down what he can.

He hears traffic in the background, and kids out front the 7-11 who are buying Slurpees after school. Blue stands up and rifles through Kevin's pockets, taking his wallet. Then he dips his finger into the blood pooling around Kevin. He writes MATTER on the wall, creating an instant altar. Honouring the god who Blue believes is changing him into what he always wanted to be, honouring the moment where he has proven himself capable of killing.

There's a story in Starling City that says if you write a god's name in fresh blood, they must come to you when you call their name. Blue will soon find out whether this is true.

He stops into the 7-11 to use the washroom. There, he washes his hands and face, then watches his reflection in the mirror for any changes. He looks at his teeth and eyes and skin, wondering if he looks more dangerous, or at least gaunter. Then he counts the money in Kevin's wallet: There's over eighty bucks and a baggie of weed.

Blue catches the bus back downtown, swallowing hard over the lump of guilt rising in his throat, embarrassed that he feels anything at all. He shouldn't, right? This is how vampires do it: They drain their victims and steal their money to survive. Simple as that.

At least that's what Blue keeps telling himself as the bus weaves its way through traffic, brakes squealing at every stop.

23
Pacts

It surprises Julie when Blue walks into the pub and takes a seat at the bar. He orders a half liter of red wine. Julie is busy with a table, her last customers for the day. She stops at the bar on her way to the kitchen with a stack of dirty plates on her arm.

"I thought we were meeting later," she says. They have plans to go out to the clubs, but there are hours to go before any are open.

"I wanted to surprise you," Blue says. He takes a big gulp of wine and refills his glass. His hands are shaking.

"Is everything okay?"

"Yeah," Blue says. "Things might actually be great, but I'll tell you why later."

A bell rings in the background: Food's up. "I gotta go," Julie says. "I'll be done in another fifteen minutes or so."

Blue has drained his wine by the time Julie pops up beside him again. "Ready to go?" she asks.

Outside, the sky is turning overcast. People honk at each other from their cars, eager to get home from work. A ghost comes running up to Blue and Julie. The spectre is nothing but long brown hair and sunken eyes. It yells: "Do it to me! Do it to me!"

Blue licks his lips. Wine has stained them purple. "Do what?" he asks.

"Free me! Make me a god."

The ghost is shouting over the blare of traffic, its voice carrying all the way down the block. People turn to look. At the corner, a spirit looks up from a garbage can it is digging through. "Do it to me, too!" the trash can ghost says, hobbling over towards Blue and Julie.

"We saw Him last night!" the brown-haired ghost says. "Matter. He was here. Without you. He doesn't need you anymore."

"He doesn't need anyone anymore!" the other spirit hisses.

"No prayers."

"No chains."

"He roams! He does what you once did for Him: He gathers a new cult."

"Now do it to us! We can teach you things, too. We know these streets better than anyone. We can show you the real magic that fell between the cracks of the sidewalks where no one ever bothered to look for it. Potent stuff."

Blue and Julie just keep walking. "Ignore them," Blue whispers, but the ghosts follow, breathing into their ears, tapping at their shoulders until they get within a few blocks of Julie's apartment before finally giving up.

Inside, Julie turns the stereo on before changing out of her clothes. "Do you mind if I grab a quick shower?"

"Can I join you?" Blue asks. He can't seem to shake the feeling of dirty hands. He went to the bathroom at the pub twice, scrubbing furiously, but still doesn't feel clean enough.

The water pressure at Julie's apartment is stronger than what Blue has at home. The steam rises around them. Julie leans against the wet tiles and reaches out to Blue, puts her hands around his back and pulls him to her. Their mouths meet, filling with water and the lather of their shampoo. Julie drops to her knees and takes Blue into her mouth. He grabs at her hair, taking a wet handful. He comes fast and lets loose a sound from his throat that is halfway between a sob and a laugh.

Julie is toweling off when Blue picks her up and carries her to the bedroom. Her toe catches on a splinter in the doorframe. She swears, but tries not to let it bother her. "Sorry," Blue says, pinching the splinter between his fingers. "Way to kill the moment, huh?" he gets the sliver out of Julie's skin and kisses the small bead of blood that wells up there. Julie kisses him back, opening herself beneath him, wrapping her legs around his waist.

After, they let their hair dry into Julie's pillows, smoking cigarettes and staring at the ceiling until they fall asleep.

The sun is finally going down when they wake up. The CD Julie put on the stereo stopped long before. She gets up to play it again and Blue looks at his clothes on the floor.

"Any chance you have some jeans and a t-shirt I can borrow for tonight?" he asks. Julie points to a dresser drawer. She goes through her closet and pulls out a tight black dress, something she has only worn twice before. It hugs her body and shows every curve. The hem comes to sit below her ass—not an inch more. Before, she always felt too exposed when she wore it. But today, it takes on new meaning as Julie imagines herself dancing in it later, a new power moving through her body.

"What did you want to tell me earlier?" Julie asks, leaning into her mirror to put on a fresh coat of eyeliner.

Blue looks at his hands again. Are they still red? Are there still stains in the whorls of his fingertips? No, just a trick of the light.

"Oh, I was going to ask you if you'd heard about the spell where you write a god's name in fresh blood and they will come whenever you call them. But it has to be the blood of someone you've killed."

Julie contemplates her reflection in the mirror. Behind her, Blue's expression is full of strange potions that play across his eyes.

"I don't think I've heard that," Julie says. "But we don't need to kill anyone, do we? Matter already came to us."

"True," Blue says. "But where is He now? The ghosts said they saw Him. That's He's on his own."

"So you want to kill someone to make Him stay?" Julie asks.

"Well, it's what vampires do anyway, isn't it? They kill people."

Julie runs a tube of lipstick over her lips. She tugs at her hair. It's a mess from sleeping on it wet, but a little hairspray will fix that.

"I guess so," she says. "But vampires don't always take lives. Sometimes they just take what they need instead: Just enough blood to get by. Or they even take their victims as lovers. That would be cool, wouldn't it? Or do you just want it to be the two of us, forever and ever?" She turns away from the mirror now and stretches across the bed. Blue pulls on a clean black t-shirt he's found in Julie's drawer.

"I already did it, Julie," Blue says as his head pops out of the shirt's collar. "I killed someone today."

Julie sits up. "You're joking," she says.

"It was Kevin Dyer. We were friends. Well, kind of. I mean, I knew him. It just happened. I was hungry. I wasn't really thinking." He doesn't add the rest of his thought: That it was easier to do than he expected.

Julie stares down at the bedspread. Blue kneels at the foot of the mattress and rests his elbows on the bed the way a child might pray to god. He waits for Julie to raise her gaze to him. When she does, she looks straight into Blue's eyes and smiles: "Cool."

Warmer nights in Starling City mean girls show up at the clubs in long t-shirts and bare legs, high heels clicking down the dance floor. Along King Street, people stop to fix their hair and makeup in the reflections of the pawn shop windows and pieces of broken mirror that residents hang from their apartment doors to ward off bad luck and ill-health.

Inside places like the Lair and the Spider and the Vixen, patrons lean against the bar, positioning themselves in ways they hope will attract attention. But whose attention are they looking for, and what do they hope might happen? Tonight everyone sips their drinks and watches the dancefloor. They watch each other, too, because a rumour has started to spread:

That there is a real, live vampire among them.

This is what everyone has been waiting for.

Blue and Julie go to the Spider first, where the drinks are half price until eleven. A black cat runs into the club when the door opens. It slinks between people's legs and runs scared across the dance floor. Julie bends down and tries to call it over but it only flattens its ears against the music and hides behind an old sofa near the back.

"Wanna dance?" Blue asks, and Julie gets up and moves toward the dancefloor. There's a throb in her foot where the splinter went in earlier.

The music at the Spider is always good, but the place is small. It used to be a crammed convenience store. The bar is the old checkout counter with the original cash register, which has been painted black and covered in stickers from every band that's travelled in and out of town since this place opened.

Blue and Julie move their bodies close together. The cat sneaks up between them, braver now. Julie bends down to pick it up. Her and Blue cradle it between each other. Someone snaps a picture. The flash is white and clear, and for a second, everyone's true faces are revealed without the game of shadow and coloured lights.

Just before eleven they head over to the Lair. That's where they find Matter. He's dancing, holding someone close as he sways. Now He's tipping his dance partner over, dipping her to taste from her neck. She goes limp in His arms. Her hands are grazing the wet floor. He carries her to a booth nearby. A few others are there, too. All asleep, or unconscious. Or dead, even.

No one bats an eye because they're all hoping to have a turn. Hoping to offer a taste of themselves to Matter. Or to get a chance to be changed by Him, invited to walk as He does through the world.

Now He's sliding into a big booth at the back of the room, the same one they sat in with Aldea not long ago. Others follow. They want to be near Him, this beautiful man who they've all hoped and prayed would one day come. Three women rush to hand Him drinks and stroke His head and legs. The grit of the city rests on the corners of each girl's mouth and the candlelight from the table dances across the tiredness that's etched under everyone's eyes. Here, the experiences of everyday life have carved themselves into the posture of the people who have waited for so long to see Him.

Matter laughs at something someone says. His head tips back to rest on the velvet couch cushions. His laughter fills the room. People hear it over the music and turn their heads to look.

Jealousy flares under Blue and Julie's tongues as they watch from across the club. Blue forces himself to swallow his feelings, almost expecting his envy to turn to ash because it feels as real and dense as any food.

"Should we see if we can sit with Him?" Julie asks.

They walk over to Matter's table.

"Hi," Julie says. Matter studies her face for a moment, as though He's trying to place it. He does the same with Blue before getting distracted by a woman next to him who runs her fingers through His hair.

"Would you care to join us?" Matter asks, gesturing for them to take a seat even though there's no room left. Blue takes two chairs from another table and sets them down.

"Did you hear me today?" Blue asks. He's thinking about Kevin Dyer again, and the blood shed in Matter's name. "I left an offering for you. I called to you."

"We need your help," Julie adds. "About what we're supposed to do now."

They both watch Matter's face. The candlelight makes it hard to read His expression.

"You called me?" Matter asks. There's a small smile on His lips. "Oh no, my loves. You didn't call me: I called you. I've called all of you here." He gestures around the table, around the room. "See? All of this is my creation. My world. You were only answering a dream I wove here long, long ago."

And so it is in this moment that Blue and Julie learn it is indeed the gods who keep their own stories alive. It is the gods who have their own wishes and wants and prayers that they send out in their own ways. They call to us in dreams and dialogue and obscure omens that we interpret as personal magic. A trick to make us believe we, too, are powerful. We convince ourselves that it's the gods who need us to keep them alive and fed.

What bidding would the gods need to do for any of us here? Nothing. They are the ones we answer to at the end of the day.

"My friends! My friends! My friends!" Matter has turned His attention back to the table, is laughing again at another joke Blue and Julie didn't hear. This is the moment it should feel like it's all coming together. This is when it should feel like everything is going as planned, with Blue and Julie sitting with their maker, receiving lessons about how to be a vampire.

Instead, it only looks impressive from a distance. Another illusion to match the smoke and lights of the Lair. From across the room, all eyes are on Matter's table, everyone wondering: "Is that really Him? And who else is sitting there, so lucky to be so near?"

Like the boy who slinks over to their booth just past midnight.

There are phantoms in the wine that's being passed around the table, Blue is sure of it. He feels dizzy and possessed, capable of anything except his own awareness.

The boy stares at Blue and Julie as he walks over to them. He has narrow hips and his jeans drape well below his pubic bones. A purple lace thong rides high around his waist. He's drunk and takes the seat beside Julie, shows her the scars on his arms, mostly self-inflicted.

"Do you want to drink some of my blood?" he asks. He says his name is Star, and that he is a donor.

"A donor?" Julie asks.

Star says he offers himself up to the vampires of Starling

City: "I can always recognize you wherever I go. The glow you have before your own body decays."

"I won't decay," Julie says.

"It's loud in here," Star says. "I can't hear you. What did you say?"

Julie opens her mouth to answer, then stops and shakes her head, deciding to stay quiet. The rest of the table has scattered onto the dance floor. Sisters of Mercy blares out of the speakers, a track that has the entire club on its feet. Only Matter has stayed. He has buried His face in the neck of someone with long black hair. The perfect veil to hide His crimes. The person will be dead in another few minutes. Matter lays their drooping head on the tabletop when He's finished.

"Thank you for joining me," Matter says, standing up.

"You're leaving?" Blue says.

"What is there to stay for? There's an entire city for me, and more are waiting. Besides, isn't this what you wanted— for me to be free again, alive?" Matter smiles down at them as He says this. In the shifting lights of the club, his bloodstained teeth look black.

Blue and Julie watch Him go and then turn back to Star. "Do you want to get out of here?" they ask, and Star helps each of them up. They stand outside. Star uses the payphone down the block to call a cab, which would otherwise be impossible to find around here at this time of night.

The taxi arrives in minutes. As they get in, the ghost of a dark-haired woman appears: It's Samantha, but Blue is too distracted to see her. Only the driver notices as he looks in the rear-view mirror and sees a woman shaking her head, yelling, "No, no, no. Don't go."

"You weren't waiting for anyone else, were ya?" the driver asks.

"No," they all say from the backseat. "It's just us."

Julie's foot is throbbing when she takes off her boots up in her apartment. Blood has seeped through her socks. The wine from the club is a dream sequence. Blue is yelling at the stereo down the hall, forgetting how to push "play."

Julie hangs up her jacket and tells Star to go into the bedroom. She follows him and pushes him onto the bed. She runs her tongue over her teeth and tells them to grow. If she visualizes it enough it will happen, won't it?

"Bite me," Star says, reading her mind. Julie straddles him, pulling down his jeans and admiring the beautiful purple lace that sits over his hips and between his legs. She has never dared to buy herself lingerie as dainty as this.

"Ready?" she asks. Star tilts his head, exposes his neck. The overhead light is on and Julie can see white bands of scarred skin beneath Star's ear. She licks them, kisses them before biting down. Star breathes heavily, sighing. Julie can smell his breath.

"Bite harder," he says, breathing heavier now, clutching the sheets in anticipation. Julie gets closer, her stomach pressing up against Star's and the hardness between his legs. She hesitates a second and then keeps going. She clamps down, but it's the same as before: Her teeth get stopped by skin and tendons. Something crunches in Star's neck but the skin won't break.

"Let's wait for Blue," Julie says. Blue is still down the hall fidgeting with the stereo. Star dips into the pockets of his jeans and comes back with a razor blade, fresh out of the pack. "Here," he says, and holds the metal to his skin.

"Wait," Julie says.

Outside, something knocks at the window.

"I don't even know your real name," Julie says.

"I don't have one anymore," Star says. "I gave it away to a vampire last year. I became reborn, then."

Star presses the blade to his skin, so fast that Julie barely notices. "Here," he says, and holds himself out to her. "Take as much as you want," he says.

And Julie does. She drinks from the cut and feels caramel and copper slide down her throat. Instead of ash in her mouth, she tastes something else: a heartbeat, a memory, a desire.

"May I?" she says, coming up for a breath and taking the razor blade from Star's hand.

"Please take it," he says, lying back and sighing again.

Julie slices across Star's belly and drinks. She cuts into his nipples, his cheeks. She tells him she wants to taste all of him and she does, bit by bit.

Blue comes in and watches from the door. He walks away and comes back with a kitchen knife and a glass of water. "Hey Star, take these," he says, handing the boy three yellow pills. Star drinks them down. "Are these happy pills?"

he asks.

"The happiest," Blue says.

Star is asleep in minutes. Blue cuts into him with the knife. It goes deeper than the razor blade ever could. He follows the softest parts of Star's body and lets the blood flow. Julie laps at it like a cat. Blue follows suit. The bed fills with red liquid. It kisses their knees, small waves lapping at uncertain shores.

24
Just a Dream

Blue and Julie sleep with Star's body between them. It doesn't take long for the blood to run cold and dry sticky on their skin. They won't remember taking their clothes off and won't remember the moment they realized Star had stopped breathing. Tomorrow, Blue will say the spirits in the wine had haunted them for longer than usual.

There's a knock at the window again: a rock against the glass. Then another, and another. The sounds work their way into Julie's dream. In her dream, Julie has a fever. She is sweating it out in her bed, soaked to the bone. There's an ache in her foot that's riding up the back of her leg. Something is at the base of the bed again, sucking from the place where the pain begins. Every time it swallows, Julie hears a knock.

One, two, three, four—four more knocks before she realizes the sound is not coming from her dream. Her legs are sticking to the sheets, everything glued together with the mess that Star made.

Julie goes to the window. Now instead of a stone on the glass it's a set of knuckles rapping to get in. Julie pops the window up. Aldea is crouched on the branch of a tree. "Let me in," she says.

I'm still dreaming, Julie decides. Aldea crawls through the narrow space between the sill and the window pane. She melts to the floor and when she comes up to stand again, her long, white hair hangs down to her hips. She shakes it out, but it stays wild, full of tangles.

Aldea looks behind Julie at the body on the bed. "Oh shit," she says. "That's gonna be hard to get rid of." And then: "So where is He—Matter?"

"I don't know," Julie says. "We saw Him earlier. But He's not here."

"He was supposed to change me. He hasn't come. I've been waiting in the woods all this time."

"But Aldea, you died. We put your body back where we found it."

"But I don't want to go back there," Aldea says. "I want to be who I was before this."

"You want to be like me," Julie says. She means to be sympathetic, but it comes out with the wrong emphasis, too strong and forceful. Aldea shakes her head and reaches for Julie's hand.

"No," she says. "I don't want to be like you—you're dead just like me. Or on your way to it. Touch yourself: there's no warmth left, and barely a pulse."

"No. That's not true." It's Julie's turn to disagree.

"Yes, it is," Aldea says. "You've left part of yourself back in the woods: Don't you know that? Why do you think you've been so sick: Soul-sick, like me. Like the rest of us. You don't think you still live here, do you, Julie? In that body? No, neither of you are here anymore."

"Where are we, then?"

"Matter's got you."

Julie looks over at Blue, who's curled up like a little boy against Star's body. "I'm just dreaming," Julie says, and edges under the blanket. Everything is wet and cold. Aldea pulls the covers off. Julie's skin puckers in a response of gooseflesh as though chilled with fever. "Julie, are you listening?"

Julie sits up. She wants to grab the blankets back but doesn't even try. She needs a shower. Everything will have to go in the garbage when Blue wakes up.

"You didn't think He would change you so easily, did you, Julie? You must know by now this isn't it: That you're not even close to getting what you wanted." Aldea sits on the edge of the bed and brings her face nose to nose with Julie's. "I know what you know, Julie. You made a promise. A pact. Didn't you? You drew magic circles. You offered your blood to candle flames. You read aloud the prayers you weren't supposed to know about. Didn't you?"

Julie nods.

"Julie, what do you think happens when an old god comes to honour what you've asked of it? What do you think happens when your belief, your desire, your very being awakens something you say you've been waiting for? There's no turning back now. This is part of the pact. Didn't you know that?"

"Leave, Aldea. You're just a dream."

Aldea laughs. Her face is pressed against Julie's. Aldea has no breath, no scent, no warmth. As though she is made of nothing.

"I'll go," Aldea says. "But remember what I'm about to tell you: When you call an old god back to life, it depends on you as much as you do on it."

25
Call the Dead to Life

"What have we done?" Julie whispers against Blue's hair as they wake. There are parts of the bed that are still damp from where Star's body has leaked away. Blood has dried into their hair in thick, stiff tufts. The boy between them died with his eyes open, his mouth slack. The view of a last gasp.

"We'll have to get rid of the body," Blue says.

"But where?"

"I don't know."

Down the hall, something crashes and bangs from the neighbour's apartment.

"Let's leave him for now," Julie says. She stretches her leg, which aches up to the hip now. She stands and the pain in her foot flares up even more. She sucks air through her teeth and sinks to the floor.

"You okay?" Blue asks.

Julie waits for the pain to subside before she answers. Blue responds by coming around and tracing small circles over her back. He helps her up and runs a bath for her.

The water turns red when Julie gets in. Blue drains it and then fills the tub again. With clear water and clean skin, it's easier to see that Julie's leg is not right. There are black and blue patches all over. The spot where the splinter went into her foot is dark green.

"What happened?" Blue asked.

Julie feels tears in her eyes. "I don't know, but it really hurts." She swallows hard, trying not to cry. It doesn't work. She wipes her nose on the back of her hand as Blue turns on the water again. He gives a generous pour of bubble bath.

"We need to get you something," Blue says, pouring water over Julie's hair and rubbing shampoo into it. He is still covered in blood but will shower after Julie's taken care of.

"We can't go to the hospital," Julie says. "What if they do tests and see that we're different?"

"I know where we'll go," Blue says.

He doesn't tell Julie that he's worried about her. If they are supposed to be vampires, then how come she hasn't already healed? Why is her body decaying at all?

Blue gives Julie a little pill to take the pain away. He towels her off and carries her to the couch. "I'll bring you some clothes," he says.

Julie dresses while Blue is in the shower. He takes his time washing himself off, watching the red runoff swirl down the drain. He thinks of a song lyric he heard at the Lair once: "Blood grips the ground you walk on." Blue sings as the steam rises around him.

They don't know what to do with Star's body so they do nothing with it except close the bedroom door.

What price do you pay to call the dead to life? Star paid a price that he must have known was coming due. Blue and Julie must pay their way now, too.

They head to Jenny and Dorian's, though it's slow going. The pill that Blue gave Julie is making her feel light and easy, even though she's walking with a limp. Blue counts four dead birds on doorsteps that they pass by and Julie reads out the names on fresh missing persons posters that have gone up overnight.

Matter is making Himself known.

They stop at the lights at Barton and Main and a woman in a cream-coloured suit walks up to them. She holds out a picture: "Do you know this girl?" the woman asks. "It's my daughter. She didn't come home last night. She has friends who look like you. Her name is Veronica."

The woman's face is wet and there's a quiver in her bottom lip. Blue and Julie look at the picture, which is smudged with the woman's fingerprints, the sweat of palms worrying around the edges. Veronica smiles out at them with big, red lips. The photo looks like it was taken in a backyard. The girl looks young. She also looks like just about anyone who hangs out at the same clubs. It's hard to tell people's faces sometimes when you only see them in dark places under purple lights.

Julie thinks about the people who Matter drained at the club last night. She lets her eyes linger on Veronica's photo for another moment before looking away with a sad smile. "She seems familiar, but I don't think I know her," Julie says. The light turns green, and people brush past them. The woman says a quick thank you and rushes after the crowd, tapping a man on the shoulder in the middle of the road.

Outside of Jenny and Dorian's apartment are dozens of

apple cores, covered in ants. An empty jar sits by the lobby door. Blue opens the jar and breathes it in, tasting the energy of the scream the girls have trapped inside.

There is a buzzer for the building, but the latch on the door is broken. Blue and Julie let themselves in.

"What is it?" Dorian sing-songs when Blue knocks at the twins' apartment.

"It's Blue. I need help. Please? I have money."

"Come in," Dorian answers.

Jenny and Dorian are sitting on the floor in silk bathrobes. They've braided each other's hair. Between them are boxes of Chinese takeout and chopsticks. There's a row of empty wine bottles on the counter.

"We were just over at our neighbour's," Jenny says. "He gave us this food. Help yourselves." There's a bruise on her neck from a kiss.

Julie limps into the small apartment. The twins' faces change to concern when they see her.

"What happened?" Jenny asks.

"Sit," Dorian insists, patting the space of carpet beside her. The rug is covered in candle wax and cigarette butts from an overflowing ashtray on the night table. An athame sits between them. They've used it like a knife. The ceremonial dagger glints in the afternoon light that fights through the black lace curtains. The handle of the dagger is full of red and purple jewels that match the twins' nail polish.

Julie moves towards the unmade bed. "Can I sit here?" she asks. "Or there?" She points to a chair piled high with clothing.

"Oh, I can move this stuff for you," Jenny says, getting up and clearing off the clothes from the chair. She scoops everything up in her arms and drops it onto the floor.

Julie limps again. Her gait is noticeable.

"What's going on?" Dorian asks, popping a piece of battered chicken into her mouth.

"That's what we're trying to figure out," Blue says. "Can you help us?" He holds up a twenty-dollar bill and offers it to Dorian.

The twins clear the space on the rug. Dorian lays down a cloth covered in symbols and stars—a casting cloth, she calls it. Jenny gives Julie something for the pain in her leg, which seems to grow deeper throughout her body.

Dorian shuffles a deck of well-worn tarot cards. Jenny boils tea and pours it into four mugs.

"Drink it fast, while it's hot," Jenny says. "Try to think of nothing while you do."

The tea makes Blue and Julie feel a little lightheaded. Jenny and Dorian don't seem affected by it at all. When the mugs are empty Jenny turns them upside down and moves them across the floor like a game of cups: Whose is whose, which is which? Where will the prize be found?

Someone is walking down the hallway. They laugh as they pass the apartment door. Blue closes his eyes and imagines himself to be something hungry and ancient. Jenny and Dorian begin to hum. Dorian shakes her bag of charms and stones and bones. It sounds like the thread of tension that is running throughout the room right now. It's the sound of their minds and dreams working from the outside in, stretching out because none of them have the space within to contain all that they think and feel and question.

"Concentrate," Dorian says as she takes a handful of charms and scatters them across the cloth.

The sisters lean in, studying the patterns. Small, doubtful noises rise from their throats. Dorian pulls a tarot card. She studies its image and then shakes her head.

"Four of Swords," she says. "You've dreamt of a crypt but will be in a grave instead. No glory for your afterlife, the body encased in the cold."

"What does that mean?" Blue asks.

"Dorian's just channeling," Jenny says, answering for her sister whose eyes have become unfocused.

"This is how she reads the charms."

Dorian points to the three bones that have landed in different corners of the cloth. "See here? It means there is a body unable to repair itself. It is disintegrating, returning to nothing. Broken, it cannot last."

Blue and Julie exchange looks.

Dorian pulls another card. "Knight of Wands. Plans go to ashes." She reaches for her card deck again but Blue stops her.

"If I asked you a question, could you answer it?"

"I can try," Dorian says.

"We called Him. Matter. We did everything you told us to, and He came. He's been here, with us. But I need to know what will happen next."

Jenny moves the teacups around again before flipping them over and looking inside. She shakes her head. "He's not here."

"Where is He?"

"I don't know," Jenny says. "Not here. Gone. Or at least not with you."

Dorian clears the charms off the mat and puts them back into the bag. She shakes it up again and tosses a new handful. The same three bones scatter towards the corners again.

"Which of you is sick?" Dorian asks.

"I'm hurt," Julie says. "But I should heal soon, right? I'm not supposed to get sick anymore.

Dorian and Jenny look at their oracles, and then at each other. They shake their heads.

"There is no healing," they both say.

"But you know spells, cures. You can make people heal, can't you?" Blue asks. "I thought you were witches."

"There's nothing we can do," Dorian says. "If there was, we would see it here." She points to the charms. "The oracle has spoken. There are no further messages."

Blue stands up and paces the small apartment. The girls all watch as he leans against the kitchen counter and takes a deep breath. He looks up at the ceiling.

"Strength. We need strength," he says. "Right Julie?"

Weak, Julie can't help but nod.

Blue looks through the fridge. He finds a jar of pickles, half empty, and a small carton of cream that expired two weeks ago. He closes the door harder than he means to. It slams shut. Jenny jumps a little.

"Why don't I make you another tea?" she offers.

"Sure," Blue says, getting out of her way. He sits on the

arm of the chair where Julie is perched and whispers into her ear: "Do like I do." Julie nods.

Jenny is pouring hot water into a new set of mugs. Dorian is watching Blue and Julie. "You knew there would be a sacrifice," she says. "There always is, with the old gods. They don't come to make friends."

"They come to get what they want." Jenny finishes the thought for her sister as she walks over with a tray of fresh tea.

"You didn't say it would be like this, though," Blue says. He accepts a cup of tea and pretends to take a sip.

"How are we to know how it will be?" Dorian says. "It's up to Him to decide that. We are only the oracles, the messengers." She stares into her cup, reading the patterns of steam.

"Bullshit," Blue mumbles. He looks into his hot mug of tea and welcomes the wave of anger and fear that rushes through him.

Blue is trying to remember a story he once heard about Starling City: Something about the sacrifice of a holy woman who was destined to feed a beast. Is this a legend that's already in Blue's blood, being relived in the name of devotion? Blue stares at his feet for a moment. *If I overthink this, I won't do it. Vampires can't overthink; they must follow their instinct.* At this, Blue throws his tea at Dorian, aiming for her face. She brings up her hands but not fast enough. Jenny scurries to her sister's side: "Are you okay?" she asks Dorian.

That's when Blue grabs the athame. It's heavier than he expected. He likes the way it feels in his hands, the weight of it. Heartier than a kitchen knife, it seems to guide Blue's hand into Jenny's back. She screams.

Dorian doesn't see the attack because her eyes are squeezed shut, stinging from the hot water and the mascara running off her eyelashes. "Jenny?" she calls, wiping at her face. The athame makes it into Dorian before she can get her eyes all the way open. Blue hits her once in the back with the blade, then a second time.

He feels Jenny grabbing at his ankle, trying to pull him down—or is she pulling herself up? Blue pushes her down and drives the blade into her again, hitting below the collarbone. He hears Julie behind him, rifling through the kitchen drawers. A moment later, Julie is crouching over Dorian. There are wet sounds coming from both of the girls' bodies.

"Drink," Blue says, and Julie puts her mouth to a gash in Dorian's chest, nearest her heart. *If Julie drinks, maybe she'll get better*, Blue thinks. *If I do this and think of Matter, maybe He will help us after all.*

Blue hovers above Jenny, whose eyes are still moving, her breath shallow. Blue likes that she's watching him, seeing exactly what he's doing. Jenny's last vision as the oracle of Starling City will be of Blue drinking her blood, having become the vampire he always wanted to be.

Julie and Blue sit together afterwards. They stare at the bodies of Jenny and Dorian, who would look like they had simply fallen asleep if it wasn't for all the blood.

"They really are beautiful, aren't they?" Julie asks. The girls' silk robes have fallen open, the sashes come undone. Their small breasts peek out, spilling over the black fabric.

"What should we do with them?" Blue asks. He's made himself another cup of tea and sips it while Julie considers her answer.

"Let's put them in bed. That way they can be together, always."

They lift Jenny first, and then Dorian. Something light and gray floats out of each of the girls' mouths when they lift the sisters. It hangs above the room for a moment, becoming trapped in the black lace draped across the ceiling. There is a smell of lavender and tobacco in the air. It is the spirit of the moment, the energy of magic that can never die.

Jenny and Dorian lay facing each other. Julie interlaces their hands together. Blue pulls their satin sheets up to their chins. Julie loosens their hair so that it fans out across the pillows. "Beautiful," she says.

It will take three days before the smell from the apartment arouses any suspicion. Their neighbour down the hall will be the one to call the police. People in the building are frightened, but not surprised: Rumours fly about satanic rituals and bad people the twins were tied up with. Rumours also fly about the older men the girls accepted gifts from.

And of course, there will be other stories about Jenny and Dorian. Stories that will outlive us all. Like the one where people claimed they saw something crawl in and out of the window the day the twins were murdered—something that had no face anyone could explain.

But that's not all folks will claim they saw: While six people witnessed something crawl out of the window after the twins were killed, five others had seen Blue and Julie go into the apartment just an hour before it all happened. And that story will become the one that matters most.

26
Wizard

They flag down a taxi that's idling downstairs. Julie's dragging her leg now, and a strange colour has taken over her lips. Blue says nothing about that because he doesn't want to scare her. Hopefully the blood they drank will kick in soon.

There's still a body in Julie's bed, so Blue gives the cab driver his address instead. They can deal with Star later.

When they arrive, Blue carries Julie up the stairs and hopes his mom isn't home. She isn't, though the apartment seems to shift and settle in response to their arrival. Shadows shuffle and heave as they walk into Blue's room.

Julie can barely keep her eyes open. She sinks onto the bed immediately. It's her first time seeing where Blue lives. She wants to be excited, but she's too sick to care.

The bowl of blood that Aldea had left out the other day has dried up. It is giving off an odour and there are flies collecting around it. They buzz at Blue's ears and lips, flutter around Julie's bad leg. Blue holds his breath as he picks it up and moves it to the bathroom. He rinses it out under the taps in the tub. "Matter, if you're listening," Blue says, "we left you a fresh offering today. Two witches. You'll find them downtown." Blue waits a beat to feel for a shift in energy in the room, but there's nothing. Instead, Julie moans from down the hall.

Blue goes to her. She's pale and cold. He pulls a blanket over her, crawls in next to her. He wraps his arms around her to keep her warm. She falls asleep almost immediately.

It surprises blue how tired he is. He's soon sleeping, too, dreaming of Matter's teeth piercing his skin, and then dreaming of his body floating away.

Blue dreams the dreams of the trees outside, the ones whose roots cram up against the foundations of the old houses around here. These roots are wizards' hands, grabbing at the ankles of those who find this place, but not meant to belong here. In the dream are half a dozen pairs of hands, all digging themselves out of the earth: *one, two, three, four I declare a thumb war.*

Blue dreams of washing his own filthy hands in the bathroom sink when a beam of light comes from the tap instead. That's when Blue notices his nails have been torn off. Maybe the wizards had won after all.

He dreams of deep earth and snakes. Matter holds the snakes out to Blue. They open their mouths, jaws hinged with too much oil, dropping so low as to hit the sternum. He places the snakes inside one at a time, a jeweler laying out strands of pearls. Inside they slither on the tongue, their bodies smooth.

Blue wants the snakes to stop moving, but his jaw is locked. His face hangs open, helpless before Matter who says: "I found these for you. These are my gifts. You can't refuse them." In goes another snake, and another.

In this dream, Blue and Matter speak without moving their mouths. They put words into each other's minds, wondering: Is this your dream, or mine?

Julie dreams, too. She dreams that Aldea is kneeling next to her, telling her about God and the Devil and the Green Man and Isis and Osiris and the spirit of a wolf. Aldea keeps saying, "You must remember this." She writes a mathematical equation on the wall above Julie's head and shows her how it creates an alternative universe in the woods.

"What are we doing here?" Julie asks. "Shouldn't I go home soon? I have to work tomorrow, I think."

Aldea shakes her head. "No. There is no more work to do out there. Your work is here, now."

"But I don't want this kind of work," Julie says. "I can't breathe here anymore." And it's true: The room is going dim and Aldea feels far from her, even though she's right next to Julie. Julie swallows for air and wakes, gagging. A hair has made its way into her mouth while she slept. It's halfway down her throat. She puts her thumb and forefinger to her tongue and grabs it. Out comes a coarse, black hair—too long to be from her own head. More hairs coil around her teeth and below her tongue, seeming to spring from nowhere. She pulls at them to find more of the same, dark follicles foreign to her body. Julie sits up, swallows again. "I'm still dreaming," she tells herself as another hair tries to get down her throat. She pulls it out and gags as it comes back up over her tongue.

The light beyond the window is wrong. It doesn't come in through the same angle as in Blue's room. Julie realizes she's not there anymore.

No, she's in the house in the woods: Aldea's house, where it is always dark. Julie rushes down the hall, almost slips on the worn wooden floor to get to the bathroom. In this dream, her leg no longer hurts.

In the bathroom mirror, she pinches more hairs between her fingers—hair like Matter's. Matter, who was someone else until Aldea did her magic. Is every body a portal for possession?

Julie turns on the tap and cups her hands beneath the slow stream of water that runs yellow. She brings the water to her mouth, moisture dripping down her chin.

Behind her, the sound of horses rises from the basement. Wild horses are running up the stairs. They are running towards her. The walls of the old house stretch to accommodate their flanks and hooves. Julie runs for the back door.

The branches of the trees rustle and bang against each other. The birds fly at Julie, chasing her along the path: "Don't you know what to do when a prayer has been answered?" they tweet and chirp in her ear.

They chase Julie towards a tall old tree with a hollow in its trunk wide enough to crawl into, which Julie does, disappearing inside. The earth gives way beneath her, swallowing her whole. She is not scared, though, because the soil is soft and moist and wraps her tightly. So tightly, she falls asleep the way a child might doze in a mother's arms.

27
Fire in the Throat

The ringing phone awakens Blue. His arm reaches for the receiver before his eyes are even open.

It's Crook: "Can I score from you today?"

Blue licks his lips. There's a fire of thirst at the back of his throat.

"You asleep or something? It's almost five o'clock, dude," Crook says.

Blue opens his eyes. They ache against the light. He closes them again, rubs them with his fingers.

"Yeah," Blue says to Crook. "I just dozed off for a minute. What are you looking for?"

Crook puts in his order. He never wants much because he can't afford more than a few pills at a time. Blue hangs up the phone and reaches behind him for Julie. She's not there, either. Blue's hand sinks into a pile of ash. He brings his fingers to his face, staring at the gray-white powder coating his skin.

He looks again. The place where Julie fell asleep is nothing but ash moulded in the shape of her body. What's left is still curled up towards him.

"No," he says. "No, no, no. It can't be. Can't be real,

can't be real, can't be."

It can't be, can it? It's just magic, Blue tells himself. A trick. Matter playing tricks, maybe. Yeah, that's it: Matter has probably taken off with Julie somewhere. Changing her. Yeah, that's it. This is just another rite of passage. Julie will be back.

"No, she won't be." The voice comes from his closet. Blue twists around and sees Samantha stepping out of from behind his rack of t-shirts. "Sorry baby brother. She's gone. Just like me."

Blue opens his mouth to say something as the clouds part outside his window. A fresh beam of sunlight falls into the room and reaches right through Samantha. She disappears.

Blue turns back to the pile of ash on the bed. He calls Crook and tells him he's going to be a bit late.

Blue gathers the ashes together. He lights a cigarette, and then a candle. He goes to the kitchen and finds an open bottle of wine, half-finished. He takes it back to his room.

Blue dips a finger into the ash and tastes it. It's gritty but easy enough to swallow. He takes a fat pinch and places it on his tongue. That goes down well, too. He takes more and chases it down with the wine. He eats his way through what was Julie's entire body until there's nothing left but dust and with that, he snorts up the rest like coke.

By the end, the wine is gone and the sheets are clean and Blue's belly and blood are alive with Julie. He pats his stomach and says, "Let's go see Crook."

The Ghoul House is busy when Blue gets there. It's the weekend and people are getting ready to go out. Sandy and Troy are making dinner in the kitchen. They have friends sitting at the table.

"Hey, Blue," Sandy says when he walks in. "Crook's upstairs."

"Cool," Blue says. Sandy's always been nice to him. He smiles at her, but feels guilty about it, as though it's a betrayal to Julie. He hurries up the stairs.

Crook's door is open. "Hey man," Crook says. He's drinking a beer. A six-pack sits next to the bed. "You want a brew? They're warm but I don't feel like going down to the kitchen to put them in the fridge. Too many people are down there and it's all Troy's friends. Posers."

"I'm okay, thanks," Blue says. He pulls out the baggie of pills and sets them on Crook's desk. "It's twenty for these," he says.

"Oh yeah, for sure," Crook says as though he's already forgotten why Blue is there. Crook takes a crisp twenty-dollar bill from his wallet. "You wanna hang out for a bit or something?" Crook asks. "I was kinda thinking of seeing what Kevin's up to tonight but there's no answer at his place."

"That's weird," Blue says. "He's usually always home."

"Right? Well, anyway, if you want to chill, we can listen to some music or something. I've got this new CD—Type O Negative. You into them?"

"They're okay," Blue says. Crook puts the disc into his

boom box and turns the volume up a bit. He cracks open a new beer. "You sure you don't want one?"

"Yeah, I'm okay for now. I had this stomach bug a couple days ago," Blue lies. "I'm gonna take it easy."

"That sucks," Crook says. "I had something like that in the winter. Horrible."

Blue looks around the room. Cassie's things are still here: Her purse is under the desk, and one of her bras is tangled in the sheets at the foot of the bed. Crook takes two pills at once and chases them with his beer, which he finishes in one go.

"You wanna go to the Lair or something later? I hear there's a cool band playing tonight." Crook slurs his words, and Blue realizes he's drunk—was probably drinking already when he called Blue earlier. The pills catch up to him almost immediately—they always work faster with a few drinks and an empty stomach.

"We could do that," Blue says. "What time do you wanna go?"

Crook leans against his pillow and closes his eyes. "Mmm, this shit feels so good, Blue. Thanks for coming by. We can go whenever. Let's hang out here for a bit first. Have a few drinks. Come, have a beer."

"Fine," Blue says. He walks over to the bed and helps himself to a Coors. He opens it up and sits on the edge of the bed. Crook is falling asleep. His head droops down to his chest before he jerks himself awake again.

"Hey, Blue?" Crook says, "can I ask you something? It's kind of weird."

"Yeah," Blue says. He's watching the veins in Crook's neck, and the way the tendons flex beneath his skin when he speaks. "Will you lay here with me a second? No one's been in here since Cassie."

Blue takes in a mouthful of beer and forces himself to swallow it. The fire at the back of his throat is getting bigger, flames licking their way up the back of his tongue. He slips in beside Crook. "Like this?" Blue asks.

Crook sighs and hums. "Just like that," he says, and then he opens his eyes and looks at Blue.

Their mouths meet. The kiss is fleeting, gone as fast as a lit match. Blue wonders if the kiss has a spirit to it that is escaping into the room, freed at last. Maybe everything has a ghost, because everything dies eventually.

Crook hums again and presses his head into the pillow. Blue can see the pulse in Crook's neck is speeding up. He moves his face into the nook between Crook's chin and collarbone. Blue lays a light kiss there, and then another. Crook doesn't protest, so Blue allows his lips to press on longer. And then his mouth opens, and his teeth meet the skin. Blue tightens his jaw.

There's no resistance this time. The skin melts against Blue's teeth. The blood rushes into him, faster than he expected—so fast he almost chokes. Blue is surprised, but keeps himself steady in place. His mouth knows what to do, an unknown instinct working its way through him. He sucks and sucks, swallowing everything he can of Crook.

It doesn't take long for Crook's heart to stop. When Blue pulls away, it's just like the movies: there are two small incisions in Crook's neck, and a little blood on the pillow. Blue looks in the mirror at his teeth: in the reflection, they don't look any different. But they must be, because they worked. He did it.

He changed.

28
The Dark Secret of Another's Taste

There's a shop on Sister Street where the floorboards creak and dust covers the shelves. There are jars behind the counter that contain things no one dares to try and recognize, and the books on the shelves promise spells and potions made only for those brave or desperate enough to try them.

This is where Blue takes Crook's twenty bucks. He thumbs through a book that he's never been able to afford but always flips through whenever he's here. The book tells of ways to resurrect the dead, to summon spirits and bring life back into those who have passed. The spell calls for feathers and herbs beloved to a goddess that walks with the dead. (May she reach out her hand to give Blue something he can only dream about.) He asks for each of these ingredients from the woman at the counter. She spoons dried herbs out of various jars and lets Blue choose his feathers from a box.

He stuffs the herbs in his pockets and releases the feathers into a grassy field—an empty lot behind the bus station. He repeats the words he memorized from the book: *Tonight I seek for a mandrake to speak through my tongue. I do not draw a circle of protection for I wish to welcome the hostile. (I invoke thee.) I fall on the old knife, offer blood, exorcise the living and invert the cross. (I invoke thee.) I invoke thee!*

The sun is setting behind him as he continues to walk downtown.

There are missing persons posters up and down King Street. They cover every telephone pole. At the Lair, they're pasted just inside the door, too, and on the bulletin board by the payphone at the back. Blue stops to read them all, to see if he recognizes any of the faces. He doesn't, though surely someone will look for Julie soon enough.

Won't they? He realizes he doesn't know where she came from—doesn't know the names of her parents or the kind of neighbourhood she grew up in. He tells himself not to think of these things. Vampires must not get too attached to the living. Blue will outlive everyone he has ever known.

Bauhaus comes on over the speakers. Blue takes a seat at the bar by himself and orders a drink. He spent all of Crook's money at the shop but still has some cash from Kevin's wallet. He's taking his first sip of wine when the door opens and something like fog rolls in.

No, it's dry ice from the stage. A band is getting ready to set up. The fog went off at a strange time. For a second, Blue thought it was a spirit—hoped it was Julie.

"Is this seat taken?" A girl is sliding onto the stool next to him.

"It's yours now," Blue says.

Something taps at Blue's shoulder: a real ghost this time, but not the one he's waiting for.

"You here with anyone?" the girl asks, oblivious to the ghost.

"Not yet," Blue says. "I'm hoping a friend might show up later. But we didn't really have a plan, you know?"

"You're friends with Him, right?" the girl asks. "Matter?"

Blue drains his glass and looks at her.

"I thought I saw you here with Him the other night," she adds.

"I am," Blue says. "I was. I mean, I don't know where He is, if that's what you're wondering."

"But He's real?" the girl asks. "I mean, there are so many rumours. And so many people are missing suddenly."

"I don't know anything about that," Blue says, ignoring the images of Crook and Star and Jenny and Dorian that flash through his mind.

"I'm Tam," the girl says, holding out her hand.

"Blue. It's nice to meet you." He turns towards her now, taking her in. She flips her hair around her shoulders to expose her neck. There are scabs on her arms where something straight and sharp cut deep enough to draw blood.

"You do that yourself?" Blue asks, lightly touching one of the cuts.

Tam looks down, blushing. "Yeah," she says. There's a twitch in her eye. Her hair is thick and dark. Blue wants to dig his hand into it, feel its weight at the back of her head.

"You're beautiful," Blue says. Tam smiles up at this, shyness dissolving. She orders another round for each of them.

Another ghost taps at Blue's shoulder. It's an aggressive one. "You gonna tell me I'm beautiful, too?" the spirit nearly spits in his face it's so close. It's the ghost of an older woman in a black sequined gown. Her feet are bare and one of her pinky toes is missing. Blue tries to ignore her but she won't leave. She taps Tam's shoulder but Tam doesn't feel her.

"Everyone knows what you did, kid," the ghost says. "There's no hiding it around here. You know what He's been doing around town? Stirring up shit is what. People think us ghosts are the problem but we're not the ones running around killing anybody now are, we? But wouldn't that be nice? There are a few I'd like to pop off if I could. Can you help me, too, kid? I'll make it worth your while."

Blue drinks his wine and tries to keep his eyes on Tam even though the sequined ghost is running her cool hands through his hair. The song changes to something he doesn't recognize. The band strikes a sour chord from the stage as they warm up. "Do you want to go talk where it's quieter?" Blue offers.

Out around the back Tam stares at Blue's mouth as he talks. She's looking to see if he is what she hopes he is: Does he have the teeth to prove it? Is he breathing, or is his body animated with an otherworldly energy? Blue likes the way she's examining him: This is it, he thinks. Everything is starting to happen the way it's supposed to.

Tam comes back to Blue's apartment. Like usual, his mother is still out. He leaves Tam in the living room while he cleans out a few things from his room. He balls up the sheets from earlier and pulls on fresh ones. He lights incense to clear the smell that lingers from earlier. He gets his candles going and puts on his favourite CD.

"I hope you like the Cure," Blue says when Tam comes into his room.

"I do," she says. "Do you have anything to drink?"

Blue knows the place is dry. "No," he says, "but you won't need a drink after I'm done with you." Tam smiles at this and lets her face fall against Blue's. He pushes her down onto his bed and she opens her legs up beneath him. She isn't wearing any panties under her skirt.

Tam moans. "Do it," she says. "I'm ready." She gives Blue her neck.

He nuzzles against her. He licks at her collarbone and kisses the place where her pulse throbs. He opens his mouth and bites down. Tendons crunch between his teeth.

"Ow!" Tam says, pulling away. Blue didn't even break the skin. His teeth marks flare red on Tam's neck. She rubs at them with her fingers.

"I knew you were bullshitting me," she says, getting up off the bed and smoothing her skirt. "As soon as I saw this shitty apartment, I knew you weren't for real."

"No, wait," Blue says. "I am for real. I swear. It's worked before. Let me try again." He takes a step toward her and reaches for Tam's wrists, but she pulls away. Blue comes at her again.

"I have to go," Tam says.

"Stay," Blue says.

Tam makes for the door. Blue goes after her. He grabs her elbow. He's surprised at the thinness of her arm, how easily it twists in his grip. "You're hurting me," she says.

He wants to tell her he can't help it. That he doesn't mean to. That something is coming over him. But he can't get the words out because his mouth is working on her again. He needs to show her the truth, and even though his teeth still won't break the skin, Blue is reaching for something, anything, to keep her still. His hand finds a glass ashtray, thick enough to hit Tam in the head one, two, three times. And then her blood is flowing and Blue is drinking.

Yes, he's drinking what he needs to stay alive because this is what vampires do. "See, Tam?" Blue whispers to the girl as she takes a few shaky, shallow breaths. "I told you I was for real."

Blue is asleep when the laughter starts. At first he thinks it's Tam come back to life again. He turns on the light and looks at the girl on the floor but her body is as still and cold as it was when he went to bed an hour ago. Her eyes are open, blank. She's pissed herself, too. Blue heard that happens to people when they die. It didn't happen to Julie, though, because she didn't get to keep her body at all.

The laughter starts again. And then Blue sees her: Aldea, sitting on the floor of his closet. Her hair is longer than before—so long it hangs to her ankles. Her face is red— painted with Tam's blood. "Girl tasted good, didn't she?" Aldea asks. "Too bad you couldn't do it the real way."

"Fuck off," Blue says. He feels his face burning hot with

embarrassment. "I did it before. With Crook." He wishes his words didn't sound so childish coming out of his mouth. *What should I care?* He thinks. *I'm talking to a dead person.*

Aldea laughs again. She laughs so hard she doubles-over and comes onto her knees. Her hands feel around the carpet. She gets under Blue's desk and comes back with a piece of glass, the remnant of something Blue broke a long time ago and can no longer remember what it was part of. Aldea holds the glass to her forehead and cuts beneath her hairline. There's no blood, just skin that peels back. Aldea keeps cutting until she's gone all around her face and then pulls the skin off in one go.

It's Julie. Julie's face beneath Aldea's. Julie with Aldea's long, white hair. She's laughing just like Aldea, too.

"No," Blue says, making a move towards her but stopping short.

"That's right." Julie speaks, but it's with Aldea's voice. "Julie's with me now. He didn't change either of us and it seems he didn't do it to you, either. So why don't you come back to the house, Blue? Stay with us."

"No," Blue says. "You're not Julie. Julie's gone."

Aldea lunges at him. She holds the piece of glass between two fingers, like a claw. It gouges Blue in the cheek. He tastes his own blood. It feels like velvet, smells of cherries.

Blue pushes Aldea away. She's light, hollow. A husk of a girl. Aldea hits her head on the leg of the desk, hard. Candles topple over.

"Leave," Blue says, standing over Aldea. When her head turns, it's Julie's face that looks back at up him. Blue tells himself it's just a dream. A trick. He rubs his hand over his eyes. Aldea is back to herself when he looks again.

"Fine," she says. She stands up and walks over to Tam's body, dips a finger into the cooling blood and takes a taste for the road. "But you'll see me again. We're tied together now, all three of us. You'll see."

The problem with legend and lore is that it gets diluted over time. People remember the bits and pieces that make the biggest impressions upon them. Their minds fill in the gaps on their own. But no one can even memorize the complete story of something that has lived for centuries, lived longer on these lands well before Starling City even had a name.

The other problem is that the details of what needs to be sacrificed to the gods get mixed up with other old stories. People think it's easy to give something away. Especially to a god like Matter, who they imagine will fall in love with them, tipping them over and drinking from their necks. They imagine that this will bond them to Him, that He will be the one indebted to them somehow.

But don't you know old gods like this one manufacture those memories? Don't you know they make it so that certain details end up forgotten, left out? That there's a reason people's old journals and diaries and spell books are found with torn out pages, or end up lost in fires. There's a reason memories develop holes in them around stories like this. The gods come in at night when you are sleeping and take back the pieces of themselves that they wish to remain mysteries.

Because if people knew the truth of what they need to immolate, they might not be so quick to call upon any deities at all.

29
Remembering What It Means To Exist

It was just a dream, Blue tells himself as he wakes the next morning. He would like to sleep longer but someone's car alarm is going off across the road and he can hear his mom banging around in the kitchen. Blue looks at his clock: it's ten. Early for his mom to be up, he thinks, but then what would he know? He usually sleeps much later than this.

He rolls onto his back and closes his eyes for a minute. Is the morning light causing his eyes to burn, or is that just his imagination? And are his teeth sharper? He runs his tongue over each one. Yes, he's sure he can feel new edges throughout his mouth.

Laughter bubbles up to his bedroom window. It sounds just like Aldea. Blue looks outside and sees two women walking by, talking.

When he sits back, he sees Tam's body where he left it: *That was not just a dream.*

And then he sees something else: A long lock of white hair beneath his desk—the place where Aldea hit her head: *That was not a dream, either.*

He runs to the mirror. There's a two-inch cut in his face where Aldea clawed him with that piece of glass. *None of it was a dream. It was all real.*

"Julie's here with me." He plays back Aldea's words and clenches his teeth.

Down the hall, something clatters to the floor. His mother swears. And then there's the sound of running water.

Aldea has Julie, but Julie should be here with him.

None of this was supposed to be this way. Blue looks out the window again and asks for a sign to show him what to do. A red car goes by. A man sits on a bench and lights a cigarette. The sun comes out from behind the clouds. Blue adds it all up and decides he has received an answer.

Blue runs through the woods with the singing of a thousand years' worth of voices gripping his shoulders. The wind is at his back and the trees are rubbing their branches together as though beckoning him deeper along the path. The stars are aligned today, Blue is sure of it. The words of every spell ever spoken in Starling City are under his nails and beneath the collar of his t-shirt.

He left Tam's body in his room. He didn't move her, just covered her with a blanket and closed the door. His mother was watching TV when he left and didn't ask where he was going. She told him she was going to stay home all day, but he didn't believe her. Still, even if she did, she'd have to go out eventually for booze or smokes. He would figure out what to do with Tam then.

For now, there's a different urgency moving through Blue. He hopes he got the right things at the hardware store. But then how difficult is it to make fire? Out of all the candles he's burned over the years, all the bonfires he sat around out here in these woods long before he ever found this house. He reminds himself that flame is a birthright. The element of fire is within each of us.

The house is quiet as always. There are some crushed beer cans outside and the faint smell of cigarette smoke lingers over the threshold. Blue wonders what happens when others come here. Do they just party and leave, or are they visited by the spirits that linger in these woods, too? Does anyone else ever meet Aldea, or did she only rise for him and Julie—Julie, who knew to knock on the ground three times to wake the dead?

Just in case Julie's here, Blue walks through the house to check for her, even though deep down he knows she isn't. He would feel her if she was, he's sure of that. No, Aldea was just casting a glamour, causing a spell. Right? Still, he calls out for good measure: "Julie?" His voice is small in the house, as though the walls are absorbing his breath, waiting for life to return to this place. Blue tries again: "Julie!" He wants to scream her name, but the volume gets caught in his throat. He listens again at the way his voice sounds in the empty space. Every word—every prayer—has a vibration that never stops. Once spoken, it cannot be undone.

Blue likes the idea that Julie's name will be the last thing brought to life in this place.

He goes into the basement. It's so dark down here he can barely see. There's light coming through the little window high on the wall, but it gets absorbed by the density of this room. The place is hungry for anything it can get.

Blue likes the way the kerosene smells as it soaks into the

corners of the room. He sings as he moves around the perimeter of the room, pouring more as he goes. The song he's singing is one he danced to with Julie the first night they met. Blue's eyes adjust enough to see the patch of dirt where they buried Aldea. He douses this with kerosene, too, and then runs upstairs to do the same on the main floor. And then outside, he runs the perimeter of the house. He's singing louder now, his voice coming on stronger than it did inside. Blue is dancing and the birds are watching. He waves at them before he runs back inside.

There, he stands on the basement steps and lights a match, throws it towards the edge of the room. The fire catches immediately. He watches it for a second: the room is fully illuminated now. He looks at Aldea's resting place, half-expecting her to rise, to fight the flames that are about to consume her but there's nothing. The earth stays still. The room fills with smoke and flame. He says a charm:

The flame will heal us.
Hold your finger over its heat until you can't stand it.
Break the blister over the rocks in the river.
The water will carry the taste of you.
We will know you, then, and He will remember.
You could be in here, too. We know you want to be.

Blue runs to the front door and throws another match. And then outside, he puts more to the outer walls and watches the flames go up fast. He stands back to see the house turn orange and red and black, the flames devouring with a hunger that Blue understands.

The smoke follows him along the trail. Blue wishes it was

nighttime so the path could be lit by the fire. But he had to do it in the daytime. The omens told him so. A squirrel runs along the path. It's tame: They are used to being fed by hikers. Blue sticks out his hand. The squirrel approaches, curious. He grabs it, snaps its neck. This is how vampires survive without human donors: they drink from animals. At least that's what Blue knows from the books he's read. He brings the small body to his mouth. He sinks his teeth into it—sharp and strong. He bites as hard he can until he tastes blood. He tells himself that the more his body adapts to its new ways, the easier these things will become. Like second nature.

There's a clearing off to the left. Blue drops the squirrel and walks towards the field. Here, the blades of grass are chanting. Blue hears the same words he's spoken many times before: The prayers he repeated in his bedroom, the rituals he did at Kevin Dyer's house, the things Blue and Julie said aloud in her living room. And the names: The names of Crook and Cassie and Kevin are all alive here, too. They are the ones singing with Blue, who kneels in the grass now and listens to it all. He lets the wind brush each word over his face. He feels the fresh blood of the squirrel running through his veins. He's enlivened and sings with the sounds this field is giving him.

Blue sings songs in languages that have been dead as long as a god like Matter. He sings prayers that ask to keep him tethered to this earth all this time, to be here as long—no, longer—than Starling City itself. The world is suddenly alive, and Blue feels every fibre hum and dance in the joints and bones of his body. Beneath he feels the turn of the earth as the smell of smoke carries on the wind. He closes his eyes and imagines what will be next: the way the entire city will welcome him, the way the streets will hold him, cry for him to walk amongst their people. Blue will be a god unto himself.

The wind's direction changes and takes the music with it. The smell of smoke lingers. Blue's attention is pulled up ahead: Someone is on the path. It's Samantha. Blue walks towards her. She is shaking her head and mouthing the word, "no."

When Blue gets closer, he can see she's crying. She holds her hands up to stop him. "What?" he asks. "Walk with me. Please."

She looks at him. Her eyes seem so much bigger than he's ever seen them. He holds out a hand to her. She takes it and they walk. Every twenty feet or so, Samantha stops and tries to get him to turn around. "Find your words," Blue says, and finally, she does.

When she speaks, it sounds just like wind whipping through the trees: "If you go that way we'll lose each other." She's looking towards the clearing that leads back into McCaffery Park and towards town.

"No," Blue says. "I'm not going anywhere. I'll always be here now."

He holds out his hand for her. Samantha takes it and they walk again, but in another few steps she's gone as though the words she spoke took everything out of her.

30
Missing Persons

The phone is ringing off the hook at Barbara's. She hates it when people call so early, but she can't be mad at them: It's nearly noon.

Normally, she would have unplugged the phone by now, but she woke up different today. Last night, she took her last drink and came home. Her son used to talk to her about the magic of this city. Growing up, she always told him he was special. He was always seeing things everywhere he looked: Angels on street corners, lost souls in the hallways at school. He used to find things, too: Four-leaf clovers and lucky pennies. Barbara remembers how he would put the pennies under his pillow before going to sleep. She taught him how to press the clovers between the pages of heavy books.

That was before her drinking got too bad. It was always there, but she managed it better then. Somehow life felt easier when she was younger and still had her looks and what felt like all the time in the world to change. That was also when her son was still known as Blair, not Blue. She always hated that nickname because it was something he picked up on the streets. An initiation that someone else had decided for him, different from the name she had chosen for her boy.

But he never let anyone call him Blair after he became Blue, and even though Barbara always thought of her son by the name she gave him, she can't remember now the last time she even said either moniker aloud.

The phone rings again. Barbara thinks of the vision she had in the bathroom at the Blue Lagoon last night. She would never have believed it if it had happened to anyone but her. An angel came to her when she was washing her hands. He appeared behind her in the mirror and said his name was Star. He was dressed funny—not the way you hear about angels in the movies. This one looked just like a young man, around Blair's age. And he wore purple lace and had the most beautiful glow around him. And he said, "Barbara, tonight's the night everything changes. You go home to your son, and you don't come back here."

And then he touched her and everything that Blair had ever told her about magic made sense. She got it. Finally, Barbara felt she had a reason to change.

The phone is ringing again now. She turns the volume of the TV down. She has it turned to the news. There's a fire in the woods outside of McCaffery Park. She takes a breath and answers the phone, reminding herself the bill collectors rarely call until later in the day.

There's a woman on the other end of the line who says her name is Kelly and that she's Kevin's mom. "Our sons are friends," she says. Barbara's embarrassed that she's never heard of Kevin before, can't even name three people Blair spends time with these days. Doesn't even know how many friends he has at all—but she knows he has them, because he's always out.

"Kevin hasn't been home for a few days," the woman says. "It's not like him to stay out. He's always here. I was told your son went out with him recently. Can I talk to him?"

Barbara looks down the hall. Blair's door is closed. Kelly is crying into the phone.

Barbara looks around the apartment. She takes in the overflowing ashtrays and the piles of wrinkled clothes. At least the kitchen's clean; she made sure to do that this morning.

"I'm sorry," Barbara says. "But he went out earlier. I will tell him you called."

"Please do," is all Kelly can manage before hanging up.

Barbara looks at the answering machine. The light is blinking furiously. All probably from Kelly—the woman was trying to get through earlier. Barbara thinks of the angel from last night and plays back the messages instead of ignoring them like usual.

"Hi, this message is for, um, Blue? Hey Blue, it's Sandy. I got your number from Dustin. Um, listen, something happened. We need to talk to you. Can you call me back at the house number?"

"Hi, this is Sergeant Cairns at 22 Division. We're looking for Blue Walker. Blue, we just have a few questions and we'd like you to drop by and see me when you can."

"Hi, you don't me, but my name is Kelly, and…"

"Hey Blue, it's Troy. I know Sandy tried you earlier, but it's really important you call back. It's about Crook. Thanks."

"Hi, my name is Brian? You don't know me but I'm the

manager at the Shannon Pub. I got your number from one my staff here. She says you know Julie, who hasn't shown up for work in a few days. We can't get a hold of her. If you know her, can you have her call me? I want to hear she's okay, and if she doesn't plan on coming in again, I'd like to know."

"Hi, this is Sergeant Cairns at 22 Division. I left a message already…"

Barbara deletes every message. She looks at Blue's bedroom door again. She knows he's too old to have his mother poking her head in there. She goes back to cleaning the living room, attacking unfolded laundry and trying to remember how long it had been sitting here.

She's about to turn the vacuum on when there's a knock at the door. Barbara looks through the peephole and sees two police officers. She leaves the chain on and opens the door a crack. "Yes?"

"Ma'am, we're looking for someone named Blue. We know he lives here—is this your son?"

She doesn't want to let them in, but does. She hasn't been perfect herself and always worried that her past actions would catch up with her: Last year, she got into a fight at the pool hall and beat a woman with a cue ball. She's also been stealing from the drug store down the street, helping herself to eyeshadow and shampoo when she can't afford it. Surely they have surveillance cameras.

But Blair was always a good kid growing up. Barbara still wants to believe the best in him, though he's not a child anymore. Quiet and introverted, he's always reading in his room or listening to his music. Sure, he stays out too late, but Barbara can hardly say a word about that.

"Mind if we look around?" One officer asks. "We'll come back with a warrant if we have to."

Barbara sits down and watches the news, which has moved on from the fire in the woods. She tells herself she has nothing to worry about—Blair hasn't done anything. One officer looks around, the other asks if he can take a seat and ask Barbara a few questions:

"Where does your son go at night?"

"Where does he hang out?"

"Has he ever mentioned a place called the Lair to you?"

"What about the Spider?"

"Have you ever met a girl named Julie Decker?"

"What does your son do for a living?"

"When was the last time you saw him?"

The questions come fast because Barbara can't answer most of them. Everything is no, nothing, or I don't know.

"Hey Bob, can you come here? We got something." It's the other officer. He's standing in Blair's bedroom door. The lights are on. The cops exchange looks that Barbara can't interpret. One gets on his walkie talkie. "We'll need an ambulance."

Barbara is off the couch and on her feet now, but she doesn't stay standing for long when she sees the dark-haired girl dead on the floor. Her ankles and knees dissolve. Her angel, Star, comes rushing back to her, wrapping her in his arms and carrying her away.

31
Magic is Real

Blue sees a line of cop cars as he gets closer to McCaffery Park. The fire trucks are there, too, and the news vans. Everyone's coming to see the house go down.

"Burn the witch! Burn the witch!" Blue yells at a reporter who's setting up a live hit.

He doesn't see the pair of cops pointing at him, or overhear them saying, "That's him, isn't it?"

He doesn't know that Sandy and Troy reported him to the police when they couldn't get a hold of him at home. It gave them even more reason to be suspicious after they found Crook's body. And Blue isn't exactly easy to lose in a crowd: His hair, teased and disheveled, his leather boots, his black ripped jeans.

But Blue doesn't notice the police approaching him because he's distracted by all the spirits who have come to meet him. All of his friends are here: Kevin and Jenny and Dorian and Crook. Tam is here, too, though she's off to the side, unfamiliar with the other faces—but she'll get to know them soon enough. They're all yelling something at him but he can't hear what it is because the cops are yelling, too:

"Hey, you! Stop. Wait. Get down. Put your hands up."

Blue keeps walking, because he wants to hear what his friends are saying instead. He'll never find out because he gets tackled to the ground before he gets close enough to talk to anyone. They all watch as Blue gets handcuffed and put into the back of the police car. Jenny and Dorian wave goodbye. Crook does, too. Kevin laughs. Tam just stares. Blue wants to wave, too, but he can't with his hands pinned behind him like this, so he just sticks out his tongue and lets the streets blur by as the sirens wail.

Blue sits at a desk on a plastic chair. The handcuffs are still on. He's thirsty.

The cops know everything. They know about the fire. They know about the twins and Tam and that guy him and Aldea made a sacrifice of in Blue's room. They know about Kevin and Crook.

"Why did you do it?" The question comes from an investigator in a beige suit. Blue shrugs.

"I was hungry," he says.

"Hungry?"

"Yes," Blue says. "I'm a vampire, you know."

"A vampire."

"Uh-huh. It's why you shouldn't keep me here too long. I won't be able to live in a place like this."

The investigator makes a note. "And, Blair—do you mind if I call you Blair? We have a tip that you didn't always act alone."

"It's Blue. My name is Blue. And no, I wasn't alone. Aldea did some of it. And Julie. They're both dead now, too."

Another note goes down on the page.

"And where did you meet Julie? She was your girlfriend, right?"

"Yes, but I didn't kill her," Blue says.

The investigator raises his eyebrows and makes another note.

"So you admit to killing the others?"

"Well, Aldea did some of it."

"And where did you meet Aldea?"

"In the house in the woods. Where you couldn't find her. She was missing for a long time, you know."

"Tell me what you mean."

Blue tells the officer about seeing Aldea's missing persons poster outside a store one day. How she had been buried in that house, but he had to burn it down to keep her from coming back again.

"So you think you brought her back to life with—uh, magic," the officer says.

"I know I did," Blue says, smiling now. "My magic worked. My magic is real. I did everything I wanted to with it."

"And where did you learn magic in the first place, Blue?"

"Well, see, there's this story in Starling City that says…"

32
Julie's Rapture

Sometimes I wonder where Aldea is. I never see her where I am. But I'm stuck here, it seems. Maybe that's what happens to all of us when we die. We just end up alone, static entities that are forever tied to the place of their final breath.

The old house still stands. Blue's fire brought it down to the ground, but it came back, somehow. It's the strongest magic I've ever seen.

I don't know if Aldea came back with it, though. She had never belonged to the house, and it was never really hers—it just felt that way when we met her. But that place dates back much further than anything we can know.

I'm starting to forget a lot of names and faces now. Thankfully, I haven't forgotten Blue, but I can't remember if I had other friends and can't recall my father's face anymore. I feel guilty about that, but from the other spirits I've met down here, that's how it goes, apparently. You attach yourself to just a few memories and that's all you can hang onto.

I've tried to see Blue a few times, but he barely recognizes me. Matter has fed off his mind so much there's hardly anything left to it. He sits in a cell all day, drooling into a pillow. I do feel partly responsible for how it all happened. Even though Blue wanted this as much as I did—oh yes, we both wanted it badly. But there are prices to pay when you summon something like Matter. We didn't know it would get so out of hand the way it did, though. We thought we were strong enough for this kind of magic.

We didn't know He would even answer us. We were just going on hope.

I've heard people walking into the house. I've seen some of them, too. They have tattoos on their wrists like the ones me and Blue had—a black star and moon. People write to Blue, too. He has piles of letters he receives. Other prisoners volunteer to read them to him as they work towards good behaviour and early release.

I get wind of some of the chants that get thrown around the old house sometimes. I've also seen them being written on the walls at the Lair. Oh yes, that club is still there, and so is the Vixen. The Spider closed after Blue killed that last girl—Tam—because she was a regular there, and the owner got spooked by bad publicity. Now, those places that were so obscure before are packed on weekends—lined up around the block sometimes. Everyone wants to go because rumour has it that's still where all the vampires hang out.

But if you really want to find Matter, you need to know how to invite Him in. Aldea's not around anymore to help with that, but I'm still here. It's just a matter of time before someone finds out how to free me the way Blue and I freed Aldea. Some people have even walked over my grave looking for me, but they haven't found me yet. Sometimes I expect maybe I will get a knock, and that it will be my time to rise. For now, I'm only the faintest of ghosts. You can barely feel me if I show up anywhere.

I haven't seen Matter around at all, either. The birds haven't returned to these trees since the fire and so there are no songs to listen to, no messages carried here about Him. I don't know if He still walks the earth or if He has left that body we gave Him by now. Those things don't last—as soon as the magic wears off, the spirit's powers weaken. It didn't help that I died, or that Blue lost himself to the point of no longer being able to work a ritual at all.

Despite how everything ended up, part of me still wants Matter to live on. I lit so many candles for Him, kept His name on my lips as much as possible. That's how I will always remember myself: As a girl getting herself ready for the night, kneeling at the altar of a city devoted to the dead.

Part of me still honors my vow to serve Him, even though He left me long ago. I doubt He'll return. I'm nothing to Him dead. Just like Aldea was nothing to Him without warm flesh and blood.

But everything I've ever done and ever believed in still exists here with me. There is no actual end to life, only to the body that carries you.

> *By way of the forked path, I find you.*
> *By way of the black road, I hold you.*
> *By way of the red river, I give to you.*

Have you ever heard that charm? It's a good one. I say it

every day to keep my vows strong.

Now I know why Aldea wanted to come back. You don't know how good it feels to be alive until you're here—and where am I, anyway? Hell is what you might call it, but it's really just a place to sleep among the tree roots and the worms. Do you know how good it felt to have His tongue against open flesh—*my* open flesh? When I was still alive, I used to prick my fingers on nails that stuck out crookedly from walls—the kind that could snag your sweaters if you brush too close. I imagined these to be hungry teeth, biting, sucking. Like this city, which sucks, sucks, sucks all life away until you wish you'd never come here.

One of the first ways I learned to call Him was to pull out strands of hair and let them drop to the floor as small, silent offerings. All in His name, which you should write on the wall every morning for seven days.

Squeeze your nails hard into the palm of your hand. With every out-breath, you breathe Him: Matter, Matter, Matter.

Because once you let Him inside you, it's rapture.

About the Author

Liz Worth is a poet, essayist, and tarot reader. She has been nominated twice for the ReLit Award for Poetry. *The Mouth is a Coven* is her eighth book. She can be reached at www.lizworthauthor.com.

Previous Works

Treat Me Like Dirt: An Oral History of Punk in Toronto and Beyond (ECW Press/Bongo Beat, 2009)

Amphetamine Heart (Guernica Editions, 2011)

PostApoc (Now or Never, 2013)

No Work Finished Here: Rewriting Andy Warhol (Book*hug, 2015)

Going Beyond the Little White Book: A Contemporary Guide to Tarot (2016)

The Truth is Told Better This Way (Book*hug, 2017)

The Power of Tarot (2019)

Previous publishing credits include *Chatelaine*, *FLARE*, *Prism*, *The Globe and Mail,* and *The Toronto Star*, among others.

Manufactured by Amazon.ca
Bolton, ON